PENGUIN BOOKS

HIGH GROUND

John McGahern is the author of five highly acclaimed novels,
including *The Dark*, *The Pornographer*, and *Amongst Women*, and
three volumes of short stories including this collection. He has
previously been a visiting professor at Colgate University and
the University of Victoria, British Columbia, and a frequent
contributor to *The New Yorker*. McGahern has been the recipient
of Ireland's most prestigious literary prize, the AE Memorial
Award. He lives in County Leitrim, Ireland.

High Ground

JOHN McGAHERN

PENGUIN BOOKS

PENGUIN BOOKS
Published by the Penguin Group
Viking Penguin, a division of Penguin Books USA Inc.,
375 Hudson Street, New York, New York 10014, U.S.A.
Penguin Books Ltd, 27 Wrights Lane, London W8 5TZ, England
Penguin Books Australia Ltd, Ringwood, Victoria, Australia
Penguin Books Canada Ltd, 10 Alcorn Avenue, Suite 300,
Toronto, Ontario, Canada M4V 3B2
Penguin Books (N.Z.) Ltd, 182–190 Wairau Road,
Auckland 10, New Zealand

Penguin Books Ltd, Registered Offices:
Harmondsworth, Middlesex, England

First published in Great Britain by Faber and Faber Limited 1985
First published in the United States of America by Viking Penguin Inc. 1987
Published in Penguin Books 1993

1 3 5 7 9 10 8 6 4 2

"Parachutes" first appeared in *Encounter* (1983) and *Irish Press* (1983); "A Ballad"
in *Quartet Miscellany* (1983); "Oldfashioned" in the *Yale Review* (1984) and *Thresh-
old* (1984); "Like All Other Men" in *Firebird 4* (Penguin Books, 1985) and the
Yale Review (1985); "Eddie Mac" in *The New Yorker* (1984) and *Irish Press* (1985);
"Crossing the Line" in *The New Yorker* (1983) and *Irish Times* (1984);
"High Ground" in *The New Yorker* (1982) and *Irish Press* (1983); and "Gold Watch"
in *The New Yorker* (1980) and in *The Penguin Book of Irish Stories* (1981).

"The Conversion of William Kirkwood" and "Bank Holiday" are
appearing for the first time in this volume.

An award by The Arts Council (An Chomhairle Ealaionn) is also gratefully
acknowledged.

THE LIBRARY OF CONGRESS HAS CATALOGUED THE HARDCOVER AS FOLLOWS:
McGahern John, 1934–
High ground.
Short stories, some of which were published previously in various periodicals.
I. Title.
PR6063.A2176H5 1987
823'.914 86–15887
ISBN 0-670-81181-5 (hc.)
ISBN 0 14 01.7708 6 (pbk.)

Printed in the United States of America
Set in Palatino

In memory of
Julian Jebb

Contents

High Ground

Parachutes

'I want to ask you one very small last favour.'

'What is it?'

'Will you stay behind for just five minutes after I leave?'

It was the offer of the blindfold, to accept the darkness for a few moments before it finally fell.

'If we leave together we'll just start to argue again and it's no use. You know it's over. It's been over for a long time now. Will you please stay five minutes?' She put her gloved hand on my arm as she rose. 'Just this last time.'

She turned and walked away. I was powerless to follow. She did not once look back. The door swung in the emptiness after she had gone. I saw the barman looking at me strangely but I did not care. The long hand of the clock stood at two minutes to eight. It did not seem to move at all. She was gone, slipping further out of reach with every leaden second, and I was powerless to follow.

'A small Jameson. With water,' I said to the barman. As I sipped the whiskey, the whole absurdity of my situation came with a rush of anger. It was over. She was gone. Nothing said or done would matter any more, and yet I was sitting like a fool because she'd simply asked me to. Without glancing at the clock, I rose and headed towards the door. Outside she was nowhere in sight.

I could see down on the city, its maze of roads already lighted in the still, white evening, each single road leading in hundreds of directions. I started to run, but then had to stop, realizing I didn't know where to run. If there were an instrument like radar . . . but that might show her half-stripped in some car . . . her pale shoulders gleaming as she slipped out of her clothes in a room in Rathmines. . . .

I stared at the street. Cars ran. Buses stopped. Lights

changed. Shop windows stayed where they were. People answered to their names. All the days from now on would have to begin without her. The one thing I couldn't bear was to face back to the room, the room that had seen such a tenuous happiness.

I went into the Stag's Head and then O'Neills. Both bars were crowded. There was no one there that I knew. I passed slowly through without trying to order anything. The barmen were too busy to call out. I moved to the bars off Grafton Street, and at the third bar I saw the Mulveys before I heard my name called. It was Claire Mulvey who had called my name. Paddy Mulvey was reading a book, his eyes constantly flickering from the page to the door, but as soon as he heard my name called his eyes returned fixedly to the page. They were sitting between the pillars at the back. Eamonn Kelly appeared to be sitting with them.

'We thought you were avoiding us,' Claire Mulvey said as we shook hands. Her strained, nervous features still showed frayed remnants of beauty. 'We haven't seen you for months.'

'For God's sake, isn't it a free country?' Paddy Mulvey said brightly. 'Hasn't the man a right to do his own thing in his own way?'

'Blackguard,' Eamonn Kelly said gravely, his beautiful, pale face relaxing in a wintry smile.

'Why are you not drinking?' Empty half glasses stood in front of them on the table.

'I'm afraid we're suffering from that old perplexity,' Mulvey said. 'And we've been waiting for Halloran. He was supposed to be here more than an hour ago. He owes us a cheque. He even left us a hostage for reassurance.' He pointed to a brown leather suitcase upright against the pillar.

'I'll get the drinks,' I offered.

'Halloran went off with a boy. I've been telling them he'll not be back,' Eamonn Kelly volunteered.

I got four pints and four whiskeys from the bar.

'I should thank you for this,' Eamonn Kelly said as he lifted his whiskey. 'But after careful consideration have come down against it.'

'Why?'

'Because I've decided you're a blackguard.'

'Why me?'

'Because one must have some fixed principles. I've decided you are a blackguard. That's an end of it. There is no appeal.'

'Oh, for God's sake,' Mulvey said. 'You're not drunk enough for that yet. Here's health.'

'Good luck,' Claire Mulvey said.

'What are you reading?'

'Another slim volume. I'm writing it up for Halloran,' and he started to speak of the book in a tone of spirited mockery.

I tried to listen but found the arid, mocking words unbearable. Nothing lived. Then I found myself turning towards a worse torture, to all I wanted not to think about.

She had asked me to a dinner in her sister's house a few days before Christmas. We'd met inside a crowded GPO. She was wearing a pale raincoat with the detachable fur collar she wore with so many coats. Outside in O'Connell Street the wind was cold, spitting rain, and we'd stood in a doorway as we waited for a bus to take us to the house in the suburbs.

The house her sister lived in was a small semi-detached in a new estate: a double gate, a garage, a piece of lawn hemmed in with concrete, a light above the door. The rooms were small, carpeted. A coal fire burned in the tiled fireplace of the front room.

Her sister was as tall as she, blackhaired, and beautiful, pregnant with her first child. Her husband was small, energetic, and taught maths in a nearby school.

The bottles of wine we'd brought were handed over. Glasses of whiskey were poured. We touched the glasses in front of the coal fire. They'd gone to a great deal of trouble with the meal. There were small roast potatoes, peas, breadcrumb stuffing with the roast turkey. Brandy was poured over the plum pudding and lit. Some vague unease curdled the food and cheer in that small front room, was sharpened by the determined gaiety. It was as if one were looking down a long institutional corridor; the child in the feeding chair could be seen already, the next child, and the next, the postman, the milkman, the van with fresh eggs and vegetables from the country, the tired clasp over the back of the hand to show tenderness as real as the lump in the throat, the lawnmowers in summer, the thickening waists. It hardly seemed necessary to live it.

'What did you think of them?' she'd asked as she took my arm in the road outside.

'I thought they were very nice. They went to a great deal of trouble.'

'What did you think of the house?'

'It's not my kind of house. It's the sort of house that would drive me crackers.'

'What sort of house would you like?'

'Something bigger than that. Something with a bit more space. An older house. Nearer the city.'

'Excuse me,' she said with pointed sarcasm as she withdrew her arm.

I should have said, 'It's a lovely house. Any house with you would be a lovely house,' and caught and kissed her in the wind and rain. And it was true. Any house with her would have been a lovely house. I had been the fool to think that I could stand outside life. I would agree to anything now. I would not even ask for love. If she stayed, love might come in its own time, I reasoned blindly.

'Do you realize how rich the English language is, that it should have two words, for instance, such as "comprehension" and "apprehension", so subtly different in shading and yet so subtly alike? Has anything of that ever occurred to you?' This was Mulvey now.

'No, I hadn't realized.'

'Of course you wouldn't. And I'd rather comprehend another drink.'

'Comprehension. Apprehension.' Eamonn Kelly had started to say as I went to get the drinks. 'I'll apprehend you for a story. An extraordinarily obscene story.'

'Jesus,' Mulvey groaned.

'I hope it's not long,' Claire Mulvey said. 'Where have you been all this time?' she asked as he began. 'We don't have to listen to that. Those stories are all the same.'

'I got mixed up with a girl.'

'Why didn't you bring her here? You should at least have given us the chance to look her over.'

'She wouldn't like it here. Anyhow it's over now.'

'I'm glad you're here,' she said.

'Is he?' Eamonn Kelly shouted, annoyed that we hadn't listened to the story he'd been telling.

'Is he what?' Mulvey asked.

'Is he here? Am I here?'

'Unfortunately you're here,' Mulvey replied.

'Hypocrites. Liars.'

'Lies are the oil of the social machinery.'

'Don't mind him,' Mulvey said.

'Lies,' he ignored. 'She ate green plums. She was pregnant. That's why she's not here. Blackguard.'

'This is terrible,' Mulvey said.

The anxiety as to where she was at this moment struck without warning. 'Did you ever wish for some device like radar that could track a person down at any given moment, light up where they were, like on a screen?' I turned to Mulvey.

'That would be a nightmare.' Mulvey surprisingly rallied to the question, his interest caught. 'I was never very worried about what other people were up to. My concern has always been that they might discover what *I* was up to.'

'Then you've never loved,' Eamonn Kelly said grandly. 'I know what he's talking about. There were times I too wished for radar.'

'I wouldn't mind putting radar on Halloran just now. To get him to give me that cheque. To give him back his damned suitcase. We've ferried the thing around for two whole days now,' Mulvey turned aside to complain.

'You must have wanted to know sometimes what I was doing,' Claire Mulvey said.

'Never.'

'Even if that is true, I don't think you should say it.'

'That's precisely why it should be said. Because it is true. Why else should anything be said?'

They started to quarrel. I bought a last round. It was getting close to closing time. Eamonn Kelly had begun an energetic conversation with himself, accompanied by equally vigorous gestures, a dumbshow of removing hat and gloves, handshakes, movements forward and back, a great muttering of some complicated sentence, replacing of hat and gloves. The Mulveys had retreated into stewing silences. I was bewildered as to what I was doing here but was even blinder still about possible alternatives. A whole world had been cut from under me.

'Do you have enough for a sugar bag?' Mulvey suddenly asked. 'We could go back to my place.'

'I have plenty.'

'I'll make it up to you as soon as I see Halloran.'

The sugar bags were strong grey paper bags used to take bottles of stout out. They usually held a dozen. I bought three. Eamonn Kelly assumed he was going back to Mulvey's with us, for he offered to carry one of the bags. Claire Mulvey carried Halloran's suitcase. There were many drunks on the street. One made a playful pass at the sugar bag Mulvey carried, and got berated, the abuse too elevated and fluent to get us into trouble. We could not have looked too sober ourselves, for I noticed a pair of guards stand to watch our progress with the case and sugar bags. Mulvey's house was in a terrace along the canal. A young moon lay in a little water between the weeds and cans and bottles.

'The wan moon is setting on the still wave,' Eamonn Kelly took up from the reflection as he swayed along with a sugar bag.

'Burns,' Mulvey said savagely. 'And there's not a wave in sight. What do you think of old Burns?' he said as he put the key in the door.

A red-eyed child in a nightdress met us. She was hungry. Claire Mulvey soothed her, started to get her some food from the cold press, and we took the sugar bags upstairs. There was no furniture of any kind in the room other than empty orange crates. There were plenty of books on the floor along the walls. The room was chilly, and Mulvey stamped on some of the orange crates until they were broken enough to fit into the grate. He lit them with newspaper and they quickly caught.

Eamonn Kelly was busy opening the bottles with a silver penknife. When Claire Mulvey joined us he had opened all the bottles in one of the sugar bags. The orange boxes had all burned down, taking the chill from the room, leaving delicate traceries of blackened wire in the grate.

'She's gone to sleep again. There was some milk and cereal,' Claire Mulvey said.

We drank steadily. Eamonn Kelly opened more bottles. Mulvey lectured Kelly. Then he lectured me. The toilet in the corridor didn't work. I fought sleep.

The room was full of early light when I awoke. I'd been placed on a mattress and given a pillow and rug. There was nobody else in the room. The books were scattered all along the walls. Empty bottles were everywhere, the room filled with the sour-sweet odour of decaying stout. The shapes of blackened wire stood in the empty grate.

It was the first morning without her, and I could hardly believe I'd slept. I got up, picked my way between the bottles to the outside toilet that didn't work, ran the water in the sink, picked my way back to the mattress. The palest of crescent moons still lay on the dirty water of the canal.

Church bells started to beat the air. It was Sunday – seven o'clock. I got up and let myself out of the house. Everywhere people were going to Mass. I drifted with them as far as the church door, turning back into the empty streets once Mass had started, walking fast until I came to a quiet side street where I sat on the steps of one of the houses. There were five steps up to each house. The stone was granite. Many of the iron railings were painted blue. Across the street was a dishevelled lilac bush. They'd taught us to notice such things when young. They said it was the world. A lilac bush, railings, three milk bottles with silver caps, granite steps. . . . I had to rise and walk to beat back a rush of anger. I'd have to learn the world all over again.

The Mulveys were sitting round the table in the kitchen when I got back. The child was eating cereal, the parents drinking tea from mugs.

'I'm sorry I passed out last night.'

'It's all right. You were tired,' Mulvey smiled – often he could be charming in the morning.

'Did Kelly go home?'

'He always goes home no matter how drunk he is.'

I handed round newspapers I'd bought on the way back and was given tea. The child inspected me gravely from behind her spoon.

'Can you lend me a fiver?' Mulvey asked me about midday.

'I'll give it back to you as soon as I find Halloran.'

'You don't have to worry about that.' It was a sort of freedom to be rid of the money.

'There's no reason I should be spending all your money. I'll give it back to you this evening. We're bound to unearth Halloran this evening,' and the rest of the day was more or less arranged. We had drinks at a tiny local along the canal, the child had lemonade and crisps.

Stew was heated when we got back to the house. Then Mulvey shut himself upstairs to write a review. Claire Mulvey watched an old movie with Cary Grant on the black-and-white television. I played draughts with the child. It was four when Mulvey came down.

'How did it go?' I asked without looking up from the pieces on the board.

'It didn't go at all. I couldn't get started with thinking of that damned Halloran. He's ruined the day as well.' He was plainly in foul humour.

We left the child to play with neighbours and set out towards Grafton Street to look for Halloran, Mulvey carrying the suitcase. He had been at his most affable and bluff-charming while handing over the child to the neighbours, but as soon as we were alone he started to seethe with resentment.

'It's an affront to expect someone to lug this thing round for two whole days.'

'What harm is it?' his wife made the mistake of saying. 'He's not a very happy person.'

'What do you know about his happiness or unhappiness?'

'He sweats a kind of unhappiness. He's bald and huge and not much more than thirty.'

'I never heard such rubbish. He's probably in some good hotel down in Wicklow at this very moment, relaxing with a gin and tonic, watching the sun set from a deckchair, regaling this boy with poetry or love or some other obscenity. I'm not carrying the fat ponce's suitcase a yard farther,' and he flung it from him, the suitcase sliding to a violent stop against the ledge of the area railing without breaking open.

'I'll carry it.' His wife went and picked up the case, but Mulvey was already striding ahead.

'When we were first together I used to hate these rows. I used to be ill afterwards, but Paddy taught me that there was nothing bad about them. He taught me that fights shouldn't be taken too seriously. They often clear the air. They're just another form of expression,' she confided.

'I hate rowing.'

'I used to feel that way!'

This, I thought, was a true waste. If she was with me now we could be by the sea.

But we'd gone to the sea four Sundays before, to Dollymount. She'd been silent and withdrawn all that day. I was afraid to challenge her mood, too anxious just to have her near, to follow her anywhere. She said we'd go over to the sandhills on the edge of the links, away from the wall and the crowded beach. She seemed to be searching for a particular place among the sandhills, and when she found it smiled that familiar roguish smile I hadn't seen for months, and took a photo from her handbag.

'Willie Moran took that on this very spot,' she said. 'Do you recognize it at all?'

Willie Moran was a young solicitor she'd gone out with. She'd wanted to marry him. It had ended a few months before we met. After it ended she hadn't been able to live alone and had gone back to an older sister's house.

I used to be jealous of Willie Moran but by now even that had been burned away. I just thought him a fool for not marrying her, wished that I'd been he. I handed her back the photo. 'You look beautiful in it.'

'You see, it was afterwards it was taken. I'm well tousled.' She laughed and drew me down. She wanted to make love there. There seemed to be no one passing. We covered ourselves with a white raincoat.

Her mood changed as quickly again as soon as we rose. She wanted to end the day, to separate.

'We could go to one of the cinemas in O'Connell Street or to eat somewhere.' I would offer anything to keep her near.

'No. Not this evening. I just want to have an early night. I've a kind of headache.'

It was then she pointed out that she'd lost an earring in the sandhills, one of a pair of silver pendants I'd given her for her birthday.

As soon as she left me I retracked my way back into the sandhills. Our shapes were still where we had lain in the loose sand. With a pocket comb I came on the pendant where the sand and long white grass met. I was very happy, only too anxious to believe that it augured well, that it was a sign that the whole course of the affair had turned towards an impossible happiness. 'We will be happy. We'll be happy. It will turn out all right now.' It was a pure dream of paradise.

But all the finding of the pendant had done was to hold off this hell for four whole weeks. It was strange to think that but for coming on the simple earring in the sand, this day, this unendurable day, would have fallen four weeks ago. She had said so.

The Harcourt Street lights had brought Mulvey's enraged stride to a stop. He turned and came back towards us. 'If I can't carry it, it's an even worse form of humiliation to have to watch my wife carry it. Throw it there,' and when she protested he took it from her and threw it down.

'I'll carry it,' I said. It was so light it could be empty, but when I swung it I felt things move within the leather.

'What business of yours is it?' he demanded.

'None. But I don't want to leave it behind on the street.'

'You take it too seriously.' He brightened. 'It wouldn't be left behind.'

'I don't mind carrying it at all,' I said.

'Do you know what colour of sky that is?' He pointed above the roofs of Harcourt Street.

'It's blue,' I said. 'A blue sky.'

'It's not a blue sky, but it goes without saying that blue is what it would be called by everybody in this sloppy country. *Agate* is the exact word. There are many blues. That is an agate sky.'

'How do you know it's agate?'

'A painter I used to knock around with taught me the different colours.'

'It's a beautiful word,' I said.

'It's the *right* word,' he replied.

'I've just noticed what a lovely evening it is,' Claire Mulvey said wistfully. 'There's just the faintest hint of autumn.'

'The last time we met I seem to remember you saying that Halloran was all right,' I said. 'You said he was a sensitive person.'

'Oh, I was just making him up,' Mulvey laughed, breaking as quickly into jocular good humour as he had into anger. 'You don't have to take what I say about people so solemnly. I am always making people up. People need a great deal of making up. I don't see how they'd be tolerable otherwise. Everybody does it. You'll learn that soon enough.'

The light seemed to glow in a gentle fullness on the bullet-scarred stone of the College of Surgeons. Stephen's Green looked full of peace within its green railings. There was a smoky blue in the air that warned of the autumn. Claire Mulvey had been silent for several minutes. Her face was beautiful in its tiredness, her thoughts were plainly elsewhere.

'We have to be thankful for this good weather while it lasts,' she said when we reached the bar. 'It's lovely to see the doors of the bars open so late in the summer.'

Halloran was not in the bar. We counted out the money and found we'd enough for one round but not for a second. Mulvey bought the drinks and took them to a table near the door. We could see the whole way across the street to the closed shoeshop.

'Where's that case?' Mulvey said in an exasperation of waiting. 'We've been lugging it around for so long we might as well see what we've been lugging around.'

'What does it matter? He left it with us,' Claire Mulvey pleaded. 'And he may come at any minute.'

The opposition seemed to drive Mulvey on. When the lock held, he lifted the suitcase to his knees and, holding it just below the level of the table, took a nail file from his pocket.

'Don't open it,' his wife pleaded. 'He left it locked. It's like opening someone's letters.'

Suddenly the lock sprung beneath the probing of the small file, and he opened it slowly, keeping one eye on the door. An assortment of women's underclothes lay in the bottom of the case, all black: a slip, a brassière, panties, long nylon stockings; a pair of red shoes; and beneath, a small Roman Missal, its ribbons of white and green and yellow and red hanging from the edges. *In Latin and English for every day in the year.*

I thought he'd make a joke of it, call to have a bucket of water in readiness when Halloran appeared with the boy. 'This is just too much,' he said, and closed the suitcase, probing again with the nail file till the catch locked.

'It wasn't right to open it,' Claire Mulvey said.

'Of course it was right. Now we know what we're really dealing with. Plain, dull, unimaginative perversity. Imagine that ponce dressing himself up in the gear. It's too much.'

'It mightn't be his,' she protested.

'Of course it's his. Whose else could it be!'

Eamonn Kelly came in. He'd met Halloran and the boy in Baggott Street that morning after Mass. He said that he'd be here at six and had given him money to buy us drinks till he came. We all asked for pints. I went to help Eamonn Kelly bring the drinks from the counter.

'Did you get home all right last night?' I asked as we waited on the pulling of the pints.

'Would I be here if I hadn't?' he retorted. I didn't answer. I brought the drinks back to the table.

'Well, at least this is a move in the right direction,' Mulvey said as he raised his glass to his lips. I felt leaden with tiredness, the actual bar close to the enamelled memories of the morning. Everything around me looked like that dishevelled lilac bush, those milk bottles, granite steps. . . .

The state was so close to dreaming that I stared in disbelief when I saw the first thistledown, its thin, pale parachute drifting so slowly across the open doorway that it seemed to move more in water than in air. A second came soon after the first had crossed out of sight, moving in the same unhurried way. A third. A fourth. There were three of the delicate parachutes moving together at the same dreamlike pace across the doorway.

'Do you see the thistles?' I said. 'It's strange to see them in the middle of Grafton Street.'

'There are backyards and dumps around Grafton Street too. You only see the fronts,' Mulvey said. 'Yes. There's plenty of dumps.'

Several more arrived and passed on in the same slow dream. There was always one or several in the doorway. When at last there were none it seemed strange, but then one would appear when they seemed quite stopped, move slowly across, but the intervals between were lengthening.

'They seem to be coming from the direction of Duke Street,'

Claire Mulvey said. 'There are no gardens or dumps that I can think of there.'

'You think that because you can't see any. There are dumps and yards and gardens, and everything bloody people do, but they're at the back.'

'They may have come from even farther away,' I said. 'I wonder how far they can travel.'

'It'd be easy to look it up,' Mulvey said. 'That's what books are for.'

'They can't come on many easy seed-beds in the environs of Grafton Street.'

'There's a dump near Mercer's. And there's another in Castle Street.' Mulvey started to laugh at some private joke. 'And nature will have provided her usual hundredfold overkill. For the hundred that fall on stone or pavement one will find its dump and grow up into a proud thistle and produce thousands of fresh new thistledowns.'

'Hazlitt,' Eamonn Kelly ventured.

'Hazlitt's far too refined,' Mulvey said. 'Just old boring rural Ireland strikes again. Even its principal city has one foot in a manure heap.' The discussion had put Mulvey in extraordinary good humour.

Halloran and the boy appeared. Halloran was larger than I remembered, bald, wearing a dishevelled pinstripe suit, sweating profusely. He started to explain something in a very agitated manner even before he got to our table. The boy followed behind like a small dog, his black hair cropped very close to his skull, quiet and looking around, seemingly unafraid. As he came towards the table, a single thistledown apeared, and seemed to hang for a still moment beyond his shoulder in the doorway. A hand reached out, the small fresh hand of a girl or boy, but before it had time to close, the last pale parachute moved on out of sight as if breathed on by the hand's own movement.

Lightly as they, we must have drifted to the dancehall a summer ago. The late daylight had shone through the glass dome above the dancefloor, strong as the light of the ballroom, the red-and-blue lights that started to sweep the floor as soon as the waltz began.

She'd been standing with a large blonde girl on the edge of

the dancefloor. I could not take my eyes from her black hair, the pale curve of her throat. A man crossed to the pair of girls: it was the blonde girl he asked to dance.

I followed him across the ballroom and, as soon as I touched her elbow, she turned and came with me on to the floor.

'Do you like waltzes?' were the first words she spoke as we began to dance.

She did not speak again. As we kept turning to the music, we moved through the circle where the glass dome was still letting in daylight, and kept on after we'd passed the last of the pillars hung with the wire baskets of flowers, out beyond the draped curtains, until we seemed to be turning in nothing but air beneath the sky, a sky that was neither agate nor blue, just the anonymous sky of any and every day above our lives as we set out.

A Ballad

'Do you think it will be late when Cronin tumbles in?' Ryan asked sleepily.

'It won't be early. He went to a dance with O'Reilly and the two women.'

Pale light from the streetlamp just outside the window shone on the varnished ceiling boards of the room. Cronin would have to cross the room to get to his bed by the window.

'I don't mind if he comes in near morning. What I hate is just to have got to sleep and then get woke up,' Ryan said.

'You can be sure he'll wake us up. He's bound to have some story to get off his chest.'

Ryan was large and gentle and worked as an inseminator at the AI station in the town, as did Cronin. The three of us shared this small room in the roof of the Bridge Restaurant. O'Reilly was the only other lodger Mrs McKinney kept, but he had a room of his own downstairs. He was the site engineer on the construction of the new bridge.

'What do you think will happen between O'Reilly and Rachael when the bridge is finished?'

I was startled when Ryan spoke. The intervals of silence before we fell asleep seemed always deeper than sleep. 'I don't know. They've been going out a good while together. Maybe they'll be married. . . . What do you think?'

'I don't know. He's had a good few other women here and there in the last few months. I doubt if he wants to get hitched.'

'She'd have no trouble finding someone else.'

She had been the queen of one beauty competition the summer before and runner-up in another. She was fair-haired and tall.

'She mightn't want that,' Ryan said. 'The Bachelors' Ball will be interesting on Friday night. Why don't you change your mind and come? The dress suits are arriving on the bus Friday evening. All we'd have to do is ring in your measurements.'

'No. I'll not go. You know I'd go but I want to have the money when I go home at Christmas.'

An old bicycle went rattling down the hill and across the bridge, a voice shouting out, *'Fàg à bealach.'*

'That's Paddy Mick on his way home. He has no bell. It means the last of the after-hour houses are shut.'

'It's time to try to get to sleep – Cronin or no Cronin.'

It was very late when Cronin woke us, but daylight hadn't yet started to thin the yellow light from the streetlamp. We would have pretended to have gone on sleeping but he repeated, 'Are yous awake?'

'We are now.'

'That O'Reilly should be run out of town,' he said.

'What's wrong now?' I had suspected for a while that his lean, intense good looks concealed a deep stupidity.

'What he made that girl do tonight no poor girl should have to do, and in front of people too.'

'What was it?' Ryan raised himself on an elbow in the bed while Cronin slipped out of his clothes.

'It was horrible.'

'You can't just wake us up like this and not tell us.'

'It was too foul to put in words.'

'What's so suddenly sacred about words! Why didn't you stop it if you felt so badly about it?'

'What could you say once it was done? Once he made her do it. My woman was so upset that she didn't talk for the rest of the night.'

Cronin had been going out casually with a hairdresser some years older than he was, who owned her own business in the town. He was taking her to the ball on Friday.

'Are you going to tell us what happened? Or are you going to let us get back to sleep?'

'I wouldn't disgrace myself by telling it.' He turned his back to us in the bed.

'I hope you have nightmares.' Ryan swore before pulling the clothes and pillow violently over his head.

The four of us had breakfast together the next morning. There was no one else in the big dining-room except some night-shift workers from the mill across the road in their white caps and overalls and the pale dusting of flour still on their arms and faces. I'd always envied their high spirits in the morning. Breakfast was for them a celebration. Cronin was gloomily taciturn until near the end of the meal when he said, 'You're an awful effin' so and so, O'Reilly, to do what you did last night.'

'I haven't even a notion what you're talking about,' O'Reilly bloomed. He was a small barrel of a man with a fine handsome head. He had played cornerback for Cavan in two All-Irelands.

'No girl should have to do what you made that girl do last night.'

'You know nothing about women, Cronin,' O'Reilly said loudly, hoping to get the ear of the mill workers, but they were having too good a time of their own. 'Women like to do that. Only they have to pretend that they don't. Let me tell you that all women take a poor view of a man who accepts everything at its face value.'

'It was a disgrace,' Cronin said doggedly.

'You're a one to talk,' O'Reilly rose from the table in high good humour. 'Whatever yourself and the hairdresser were up to in the back of the car, I thought it was about to turn over.'

'It was a pure disgrace,' Cronin said to his plate.

Ryan and myself stayed cautiously neutral. I had clashed with O'Reilly from the beginning when I'd refused to become involved with the town football team, which he ran with a fierce fanaticism, and we were all the more cautious because Cronin usually hero-worshipped O'Reilly. In the long evenings they could be seen kicking a ball round for hours in the park after training sessions. Lately, they'd taken to throwing shoes and pieces of cutlery at the ceiling if they thought I was upstairs with a book or correcting school exercises. I was looking forward to the opening of the new bridge.

Ryan's unwashed Beetle was waiting outside the gate when I finished school at three that evening.

'I've calls in the Gaeltacht. Maybe you'll come in case there's need of a bit of translating.'

It was a polite excuse. There was never need of translation. The tied cow could be always pointed out. The breed of the bulls – Shorthorn, Charolais, Friesian – were the same in Gaelic as in English. The different colours of the straws of semen in the stainless steel container on the floor of the Beetle needed no translation. Ryan just didn't like driving on the empty roads between these silent, alien houses on his own.

'I got the whole business out of Cronin in the office this morning.' A wide grin showed on his face as the VW rocked over the narrow roads between the bare whitethorns.

'What was it, then? I guarantee you I won't be shocked.'

'It shocked Cronin.'

'What was it, for Christ's sake?'

'O'Reilly got Rachael to take his lad in her mouth,' Ryan said. 'Then he wouldn't let her spit it out.'

'Spit out what?'

'What's in the bucket,' he gestured towards the bright steel container on the floor of the VW where the straws were kept in liquid nitrogen.

'They say it's fattening,' I said ironically to hide my own sense of shock.

'Not half as fattening as in the other place.' I was unprepared for the huge roar of laughter my poor irony induced.

'What do you mean?'

'O'Reilly's in a white fright. He's got Rachael up the pole.'

'Then he'll marry her.'

'Not unless he has to. Cronin told me that he spent all last week applying for engineering jobs in South Africa. It seems they're building lots of bridges in South Africa.'

'But he has a permanent job to go to in Galway as soon as the bridge finishes. He's been boasting about it long enough.'

'He could go if he married Rachael, but it mightn't be so easy if he refused to do the decent. News travels.'

We'd come to the first of the plain ugly cottages the government had built on these twenty-acre farms. They were all alike. A woman met us, showed us to the cow, gave Ryan a basin of hot water, soap, a towel to wash and dry his rubbered arm afterwards. She responded to my few questions with deep suspicion, fearful that I was some government official sent out to check on grants or the speaking of Irish.

These people had been transplanted here from the seaboard as part of de Valera's dream; lighthouses put down on the plain from which Gaelic would spread from tongue to tongue throughout the land like pentecostal flame. Used to a little fishing, a potato patch, grass for a cow between the rocks, they were lost in the rich green acres of Meath. A few cattle were kept knee-deep in grass, or the land was put out on conacre to the grain contractors who supplied the mill – and the men went to work in England. It was dark by the time we'd finished. The last call had to be done by the light of a paraffin lantern.

'What will Rachael do if O'Reilly ditches her?' I asked as we drove back.

'What does any girl do? She has to nail her man. If she doesn't. . . .' He spread his hands upwards underneath a half-circle of the steering wheel. 'You might as well come to the ball. It'll be twice as much fun now that we know what's afoot.'

'I'll not go. For me it's just another reason to stay away.'

The dress suits came in flat cardboard boxes on the evening bus the Friday of the ball. Tulips came in similar boxes for the altar. O'Reilly changed into his suit as soon as he came home from work and went to the hotel to have drinks with sub-contractors on the bridge. There had plainly been a falling out between himself and Cronin. Ryan and Cronin waited till after tea to change. They'd never worn dress suits before and were restless with excitement, twisting themselves in mirrors, laughing nervously as they paraded in front of the McKinneys. They found time slow to pass before they'd to go for their girls. Having no steady girl, Ryan was bringing the girl who took the calls in their office. I went with them to the Midland's Bar, where we had three rounds of hot whiskeys. Still it wasn't late enough to leave when we got back, and they went alone to some other bar, this time taking their cars. O'Reilly had taken his car to the hotel. I'd meant to read, but when left alone I found that I wasn't able to because of the excitement and the whiskey. I was half-tempted to go back up to the Midland's with old Paddy McKinney when he went for his nightly jar, and glad when Mrs McKinney came in soon afterwards to join me at the fire.

'You didn't go to the ball after all?'

'No. I didn't go.'

'You may be as well off. Old Paddy was a great one for dances and balls in his day, would never miss one. And he got me. And I got him. That's all it ever seems to have amounted to,' she said with vigorous incomprehension. Later I tried to ask her if she'd let me have O'Reilly's room when he left, but she'd give no firm answer, knowing it'd be easier to let the room than to fill the bed in the upstairs room, and, as if to make up for her evasion, she made delicious turkey sandwiches and a big pot of tea instead of the usual house glass of milk and biscuits.

The screeching of a car to a violent stop beneath the window woke me sometime in the morning. A door banged but I could hear no voices. A key turned in the front door. I sat up as footsteps started to come up the stairs. O'Reilly opened the door. His oiled hair was dishevelled as was the suit and bow.

'I want you to convey a message for me when they return.' He had to concentrate fiercely to frame the words.

'Where are the others?'

'They're still at the ball. I abandoned them there.'

'Is Rachael there, too?' I asked cautiously.

'The last I saw of her she was dancing with Cronin. Cronin made a speech. He got up on the stage for a special request and took the microphone. It was most embarrassing. One should never associate with uncultivated people. I decided that the gentlemanly thing to do was to leave at once on my own. So I'm here.' He stood solid as a stone on the floor, but it was obvious from the effort of concentration and small hiccoughs that he was extraordinarily drunk.

'Tell them that I'm not to be disturbed. Tell them not to go banging on the door. The door will be locked.'

'I'll tell them.'

'I'm most obliged. I'll recompense you in due course.'

I heard him move about for a little while downstairs. Then his door closed. I wasn't able to be certain whether he turned the lock or not.

The others were so long in coming that I was beginning to think they must have met with some accident. They made much noise. I heard them try O'Reilly's door several times, calling out before they came upstairs. Cronin was wild with drink, Ryan just merry and foolish.

'Bloody O'Reilly got home. He's locked the door,' Cronin staggered violently as he spoke.

'He was up here,' I said. 'He asked not to be disturbed when you came home.'

'Not to be disturbed,' Cronin glared.

'I'm just giving the message.'

'That's the notice he has hung on the doorknob,' Ryan giggled.

'I made a speech,' Cronin said. 'A most impressive speech.'

'What sort of speech?' I asked as gently as possible in the hope of diverting the drilling stare.

'That it was the bounden duty of every single man to get married. Of course I was referring to O'Reilly in particular, but it had universal significance as well. To show that I was serious I proposed that I myself be married immediately. This week if possible.'

Any temptation to laugh was out. It would be far too dangerous.

'Of course *you* make no effort to get married. You just lie here in bed,' he continued. The stare would not be diverted, and then he suddenly jumped on me in the bed, but his movements were so slow and drunken that all I had to do was draw my knees upwards and to the side for him to roll across the bed out on the floor the far side. This was repeated three times. 'Make no effort. Just lie there,' he kept saying, and each time the breathing grew heavier. I was afraid the farce could go on for some time, until rising he caught sight of himself in the wardrobe mirror and advanced on the mirror.

'I've never seen myself in a dress suit before. I am most impressed. Instead of giving it back, I think I'll buy it out. I'll wear it in my professional capacity. The farmers will be most impressed.' Dress suits seemed to have a formalizing effect on his speech.

I used the diversion to rise and dress. Then another car drew up outside. Looking out the window, Ryan, who all this time had stood there grinning and smiling, said, 'Rachael's back. She's looking to get O'Reilly to drive her home.'

'How did she get this far?'

'With Johnny from the mill and his girl. She wouldn't come with us. They had to leave Johnny's girl home first. We'd better go down. They have no key.'

'It is our duty to go down,' Cronin said.

I sat for a long time on the bed's edge before following them down.

A piece of cardboard hung from the doorknob of O'Reilly's room below. I lifted it and read PLEASE DO NOT DISTURB.

Rachael was sitting at the corner of the small table in the kitchen, and with her was Johnny Byrne, the foreman of the mill. She was smoking, plainly upset, but it made her the more beautiful. She'd pulled a jacket over her bare shoulders, and silver shoes showed beneath the long yellow dress. Ryan and Cronin had taken Mrs McKinney's cooked turkey from the fridge and placed it on the high wooden table. Cronin was waving a turkey leg about as he inspected himself in Paddy McKinney's shaving mirror.

'It's no trouble now for me to run you the rest of the way home,' Johnny was saying to Rachael.

'No thanks, Johnny.'

'We'll get him up now. It is our duty,' Cronin suddenly said.

We heard him rattling the doorknob in the hallway. 'Get up, O'Reilly. Rachael's here. You have to run her home.'

After a lot of rattling and a threat to break down the door, a hollow voice sounded within the room as if spoken through a sheet by a man whose life was fast ebbing. 'Please inspect notice and go away,' at which point Rachael went out and ushered Cronin back into the kitchen. He was amazingly docile in her hands. Ryan was peeling the turkey breastbone clean with his fingers.

'You must leave him alone. It's between us,' Rachael moved him gently back towards the turkey on the table.

'Even if you got him up now he'd hardly be fit to drive you home,' Johnny Byrne said.

'We could give him coffee,' and after a time she added, 'I'll try just once more.' She called him, asking him to let her into the room. But all that came in the silence were loud, simulated snores.

'It'd only take a minute to run you home,' Johnny said when she came back into the kitchen.

'No, Johnny. I'll wait. You should go home now. You won't mind till you have to go to work,' and reluctantly, pausing a number of times, he rose and left. Having stripped the turkey clean, Cronin and Ryan fell asleep in chairs. In the garishly lit kitchen, I sat in Byrne's place at the table. A foolish, sentimental, idle longing grew: to leave her home, to marry her, to bring up O'Reilly's child with her in some vague, long vista of happiness; and after an hour I said, 'I could get one of their car keys', indicating the sleeping inseminators, 'and drive you home.'

'No,' she said firmly. 'I'll wait now till morning.'

She was there when Mrs McKinney came down to get the breakfasts in the morning, there to face her bustling annoyance at the disturbances of the rowdy night turn to outrage at the sight of the pillaged turkey on the table.

'I'm sorry to be here. I'm waiting for Peter to get up. He was drunk and locked the door. He took me to the dance and he has to take me home,' she explained with a quiet firmness.

'Was it him did for the turkey too?' The old woman made no effort to conceal her anger.

'No. I don't think so.'

'It must be those other bowsies, then.'

In her long yellow dress and silver shoes Rachael helped tidy the kitchen and prepare for the breakfasts until the old woman was completely pacified, and the two sat down like ancient allies to scalding tea and thickly buttered toast. Through the thin wall they heard O'Reilly's alarm clock go off.

'They're not worth half the trouble they put us to,' the old woman grumbled.

They heard him rise, unlock the door, go upstairs to the bathroom, and as he came down Rachael went out to meet him in the hallway. It was several minutes before she returned to the kitchen, and then it was to borrow a kettle of boiling water. Outside on the street it was a white world. The windscreen of O'Reilly's car was frosted over, the doorhandles stuck.

'You were right to make him leave you home. They should be all learned a bit of manners,' Mrs McKinney said approvingly as she took the empty kettle back, the noise of the car warming up coming from outside.

O'Reilly was a long time leaving Rachael home, and when he came back he checked that no one had been looking for him on the site, reported sick, and went to bed. He did not get up till the following morning.

When Mrs McKinney saw the state of Cronin and Ryan later that morning, she decided to postpone the business of the turkey for a day or two. They tried to drink a glass of Bols eggnog in the Midland's as a cure before work, but it made them violently ill, and they had to go back to bed.

The town had not had such a piece of scandal since some members of the Pioneer excursion to Knock had to be taken from the bus in Longford for disorderly conduct three years before. Circling the Virgin's Shrine in a solid downpour while responding with Hail Marys to the electronic Our Fathers had proved too severe a trial for three recent recruits.

I was stopped on my way to school, was stopped again on my way back, to see if I could add anything to the news of the night, but everything, down to the devastated turkey, seemed to be already known.

Rachael and O'Reilly were married in early January. Only Cronin was invited to the wedding, from the restaurant, he and O'Reilly having become great pals again. He told us that it was quiet and very pleasant, just a few people, the way weddings should be. We made a collection in the restaurant, and with the money Mrs McKinney bought a mantel clock in a mahogany frame and had all our names inscribed on a bright metal scroll. After a honeymoon in London, the new couple went to Galway, where he took up his position with the County Council.

It was some years before Rachael and O'Reilly were seen again. A crowd up for the Christmas shopping saw them in Henry Street a Saturday morning before Christmas. They were both wearing sheepskin coats. Rachael's coat fell to her ankles and a beautiful fair-haired child held her hand as they walked. She had lost her lean beauty but was still a handsome woman. A small boy rode on O'Reilly's shoulders. The boy was pointing excitedly at the jumping monkeys on the pavement and the toy trumpets the sellers blew. Sometimes when they paused at the shops the mother would turn away from the glitter of the silver snow to smile on them both. They disappeared into Arnott's before anybody had gathered enough courage to greet them.

O'Reilly had won several promotions, and everywhere local officials gather it was heard whispered along the grapevine, as if to ease the rebuke of his rise over older and less forceful, less lucky men, that O'Reilly would not be half the man he is if he had not married Rachael.

Oldfashioned

The Protestants had so dwindled that there was no longer a living in Ardcarne: the old Georgian parsonage had been closed, its avenue of great beech trees, the walled orchard, the paddock and lawn and garden, all let run wild. The church with its Purser windows was opened but once every year for harvest thanksgiving to keep certain conditional endowments. There was always a turnout on that one Sunday, from the big farms and houses, gamekeepers and stewards of the Rockingham estate, and some years Sir Cecil and Lady Stafford King-Harmon came from the Nash house above Lough Key, in which there were so many windows it was said there was one for every day of the year.

The Catholic church, hiding its stark ugliness amid the graveyard evergreens in the centre of the village, was so crowded for both Masses on Sundays that often children and old people would faint in the bad air and have to be carried outside. Each day saw continual traffic to the blue-and-white presbytery, blue doors and windows, white walls, at the end of the young avenue of limes. They came for references, for birth certificates, to arrange for calls to the sick and dying, for baptisms, marriages, churchings, to report their neighbours: they brought offerings and payments of dues. No one came in the late evening except on the gravest matters, for by then Canon Glynn and Danny, who had retired early from the civil service to come and live with his brother, could be extremely irritable, and often smelled of whiskey. 'You could get run,' was the word that was out.

A green mail car crossed the bridge to the post office each morning and evening at nine o'clock and six. Stephen Maughan crossed the same bridge on his heavy carrier bicycle every Thursday evening with fresh herrings off the Sligo train, setting

ucycle on its legs outside the post office to shout, 'If you
i't buy you can't fry,' to the annoyance of the Miss Applebees
within, Annie and Lizzie, with their spectacles and neat white
hair and their glittering brass scales. There were two pubs,
Charlie's and Henry's, and they both had grocery stores as well.
There was a three-teacher school, a dancehall, a barracks with
three guards and a sergeant.

There was much traffic on the roads, carts, bicycles, people on
foot who always climbed on the walls or grass margins when the
occasional motor was heard. People could be seen walking the
whole seven miles to Boyle before the big matches, and after the
digging of the potatoes, when the dreaded long nights had to be
faced, holding wet batteries stiffly. Each summer Sunday the
cattle were driven from the football field at the back of Charlie's
and the fouled lines marked white again with lime. To the slow
sog of the football in the distance, handball of sorts was played
against the back of Jimmy Shivnan's forge, the bounce uncertain
because of the unswept stones, and there, too, the coins were
tossed from the backs of rulers and greasy pocket combs, each
copper row arranged so that all the harps faced upwards before
being thrown. Everywhere there was the craving for news.
News, any news, passing like flame from mouth to eager
mouth, slowly savoured in the eyes. 'Bruen's cow rolled over
into a drain, was found dead on her back, the feet in the air . . .'
'Where? When? Who came on the cow? Was she long on her
back? That'll put them back a step. It's no joke no matter who it
happens to. Terror what life puts people through.' 'A sewing
machine was the only thing left standing four floors up in a
bombed factory in Coventry.' 'Imagine . . . four floors up . . . a
sewing machine standing on a girder out there on its own . . . a
terror . . . a sight.'

Suddenly the war was over. Britain had to be rebuilt. The
countryside emptied towards London and Luton. The boat
trains were full and talk was of never-ending overtime. After
weeks in England, once-easy gentle manners, set free from the
narrow rule of church and custom, grew loud, uncertain,
coarse.

At home a vaguely worried church joined a dying language to
declare that learning Irish would help to keep much foreign
corrupting influence out. Red Algier tractors with long steering

columns and the sound of low-flying airplanes – they were said
to have the original Messerschmitt engine – started to replace
the horse and cart. A secondary school was opened by the
Brothers in the town. The word *Salamanca*, having endured for
most of a century as a mighty ball booted on the wind out of
defence in Charlie's field, grew sails again on an open sea,
became distant spires within a walled city in the sun. Race
memories of hedge schools and the poor scholar were stirred, as
boys, like uncertain flocks of birds on bicycles, came long
distances from the villages and outlying farms to grapple with
calculus and George Gordon and the delta of the River Plate.

Against this tide the Sinclairs came from London to the empty
parsonage in Ardcarne, where Colonel Sinclair had grown up,
where Mrs Sinclair, as a young army wife and mother, had
spent happy summers with her gentle parents-in-law, the old
canon and his second wife. After the war, the Colonel had
settled uneasily into the life of a commuter between their house
in Wembledon and the ministry. Their son had been killed in
the war and their daughter was married to a lecturer in
sociology at Durham University, with two children of her own.
They both wanted to live in the country, and when they
discovered that the church commissioners would be only too
glad to give the decaying parsonage for a nominal sum to a son
of the manse, they sold the house in Wembledon, and the
colonel took early retirement.
  They stayed in the Royal Hotel while the parsonage was being
restored, and as they employed local tradesmen, it was not
resented. Once they moved in, the grounds, the garden and
orchard, even the white paddock railings, they brought back
with their own hands. They loved the house. Each year just
after Christmas they went to England for two months, and
every summer their daughter and her children came from
Durham. Each Thursday they did a big shopping in the town,
and when it was done went to the Royal Hotel for a drink. It was
the one time in the week they drank at the Royal, but every
evening except on Sunday, at exactly nine o'clock, their black
Jaguar would cross the bridge and roll to a stop outside Charlie's
Bar. It was so punctual that people began to check their watches
as it passed, the way they did with the mail van and the church

bells and the distant rattle of the diesel trains across the Plains.
Mrs Sinclair never left the Jaguar, but each night had three gin-
and-tonics sitting in the car, the radio tuned to the BBC World
Service, the engine running in the cold weather. It was the
Colonel who brought out the drinks, handing them through the
car window, but his own three large Black Bushmills he drank at
the big oval table in Charlie's front room or parlour. 'Wouldn't
Mrs Sinclair be more comfortable in at the fire on a night the like
of that?' Charlie himself had suggested one bad night of rain
and a rocking wind not long after they had started to come
regularly. 'No, Charlie. She'd not like that. Women of her
generation were brought up never to set foot in bars,' and the
matter ended there; and though it caused a veritable hedgerow
of talk for a few weeks, it provoked no laughter.

'They're strange. They're different. They're not brought up
the like of us. Those hot climates they get sent to does things to
people.'

At first, the late-night drinkers entering Charlie's used to
hurry past the car and woman, but later some could be seen to
pause a moment before pushing open the door as if in reflection
on the mystery of the woman sitting alone drinking gin in the
darkness, the car radio on and the engine running wastefully,
the way they might pause coming on the otters' feeding place
along the riverbank, its little private lawn and scattering of blue
crayfish shells.

When they left for England after Christmas, the car was
missed like any familiar absence, and when suddenly it
reappeared in March, 'They're back,' would be announced with
relief as well as genuine gladness.

'How long have we been here now? How long is it since we've
left Wembledon?' the Sinclairs would sometimes ask one
another as the years gathered above them. Now they found they
had to count; it must be three, no four, five my God, using
birthdays and the deaths of friends like tracks across the sky.

'They're flying now.'

'Still, it must mean we've been happy.'

Company they seemed not to need. Occasionally, they ran
into their own class, on Thursdays in the Royal, after their
shopping was done, the town full of the excitement of the
market, bundles of cabbage plants knotted with straw on offer

all along the Shambles; but as they never had more than the one drink, and evaded exploratory invitations to tea or bridge, they became in time just a matter of hostile curiosity. 'How did you get through the winter?' 'Dreadful. Up to our hocks in mud, my dear.' 'But the Bishop is coming for Easter.' Mostly, the Colonel was as alone in Charlie's parlour as Mrs Sinclair was outside in the closed car, though sometimes Charlie joined him with a glass of whiskey if the bar wasn't busy and Mrs Charlie wasn't on the prowl. They'd sit at the table and talk of fruit trees and vegetables and whiskey until the bell rang or Mrs Charlie was heard surfacing. Sometimes the Colonel had the doubtful benefit of a local priest or doctor or vet or solicitor out on the razzle, but if they were very drunken he just finished his drink and left politely. 'I never discuss religion because its base is faith – not reason.' What brought them most into contact with people was the giving away of fruit and vegetables. They grew more than they could use. To some they gave in return for small favours, more usually by proximity and chance.

It was because of help the Sergeant had given with the renewal of a gun licence that they came with the large basket of apples to the barracks. The day had been eventful at the barracks, but only in the sense that anything at all had happened. An old donkey found abandoned on the roads had been brought in that morning. Every rib showed, the hooves hadn't been pared in years, the knees were broken and twisted and cut, clusters of blue-black flies about the sores. He was too weak even to pluck at the clover on the lawn, and just lay between the two circles of flower beds while they waited for the Burnhouse lorry, an old shaky green lorry with a heavy metal box like the lorries that draw stones, too wide to get through the barrack gates.

'It'd be better if we could get him alive on the lorry. That way it'd save having to winch him up,' the driver said.

They had to lift the donkey from the lawn and push, shove, and carry the unresisting animal over the gravel and up a makeshift ramp on to the lorry.

'Whatever you do keep a good hault of his tail.'

'I have his head. He can't fall.'

'Christ rode into Jerusalem on an ass.'

'He'd not ride far on this one.'

They expected the donkey to fall once they let go of him on the lorry, but he stayed on his feet without stirring while the driver got the humane killer out of the cab. When the back of the metal horn was tapped with the small hammer close to the skull, he crumpled more silently after the shot rang than a page thrust into flame. The tailboard was lifted up, the bar dropped in place. A docket had to be signed.

The Sergeant and two of the policemen signed themselves out on delayed patrol after the lorry had rattled across the bridge with its load. Guard Casey remained behind as barrack orderly and with him the Sergeant's sixteen-year-old son, Johnny. As soon as the policemen had split out in different directions on their bicycles at the bridge, Casey turned to the boy. 'What about a game?'

They were friends, and often played together on the gravel, dribbling the ball around one another, using the open gates as goal. The old policeman was the more skilled of the two. Before he'd joined the force he'd been given a trial by Glasgow Celtic. But he would leave off the game at once if any stranger came to the barracks. What annoyed the boy most was that he'd always try to detain people past the call of the business: he had an insatiable hunger for news.

'I don't feel like playing this evening.'

'What's biting you?'

'What'd you do if you caught the owner of that donkey?'

'Not to give you a short answer, we'd do nothing.'

'Why?'

'We've trouble enough without going looking for it. If we applied the law strictly in every case, we'd have half the people of the country in court, and you know how popular that would make us.'

'It's lousy. An old donkey who's spent his whole life pulling and drawing for someone, and then when he's no use anymore is turned out on the road to starve. How can that be justified?'

'That's life,' Casey replied cheerfully. He went in and took one of the yellow dayroom chairs and the *Independent* out on the gravel and started the crossword. Sometimes he lifted his head to ask about the words, and though the boy answered quickly and readily the answers did not lead to further conversation.

It was getting cold enough for both of them to think about going in when they heard the noise of a car approaching from the other side of the river. As soon as Casey looked at his watch he said, 'I bet you it's the Colonel and the wife on their way to Charlie's. I told you,' he said as soon as the black Jaguar appeared, but suddenly stiffened. Instead of continuing straight on for Charlie's, the Jaguar turned down the hill and up the short avenue of sycamores to stop at the barrack gate. Casey left the newspaper on the chair to go forward to the gate. Mrs Sinclair was in the car, but it was the Colonel who got out, taking a large basket of apples from the back seat.

'Good evening, Colonel,' Casey saluted.

'Good evening, Guard,' the effortless sharp return of the salute made Casey's effort seem more florid than it probably was. 'Is the Sergeant about?'

'He's out on patrol, but his son is here.'

'That will do just as well. Will you give these few apples to your father with our compliments and tell him the licence arrived?'

Big yellow apples in a bed of green leaves and twigs ringed the rim of the basket, and in the centre red Honeycombs and Beauty of Bath were arranged in a striking pattern.

'Thank you, sir. They're very beautiful.'

'What is?' The Colonel was taken by the remark.

'The way the apples are arranged,' he coloured.

'Mrs Sinclair did the arranging but I doubt if she ever expected it to be noticed.'

'Do you want your basket back, sir?'

'No. Your father can drop it in sometime he's our way. Or it can be left in Charlie's. But come. You must meet Mrs Sinclair,' and the boy suddenly found himself before the open window.

'This young man has been admiring your arrangement of the apples,' the Colonel was smiling.

'How very kind. Thank you,' she said.

In his confusion he hardly knew how the Colonel took leave of them, and he was still standing stock-still with the basket in his hand as the car turned for Charlie's.

Guard Casey reached down for an apple. 'One thing sure is that you seem to have struck on the right note there,' but he was too kind to tease the boy, and after he'd bitten into the apple said, 'No matter what way they're arranged they'll be all the same by the time they get to your belly. Those people spent a lot of their life in India.'

The boy showed his father the basket of apples as soon as he came in off patrol. 'It's to thank you for getting them the gun licence. There's no hurry with the basket. They said we could bring it to the house sometime or leave it in Charlie's.'

The father was curiously excited by the visit, but the boy did not volunteer anything further.

'Of course I'll leave it to the house. It'd not be polite to dump it in Charlie's,' and he was in great good humour after he'd left the basket back with the Sinclairs the very next day.

'Colonel and Mrs Sinclair have been singing your praises. They said they never expected to come on such manners in this part of the country. Of course it doesn't say much for the part of the country.'

'I only thanked them for the apples.'

'They said you remarked on how the apples were arranged. You certainly seemed to have got above yourself. I kept wondering if we were talking about the same person. They want to know if you'd help them in the garden for a few hours after they come back from England.'

'What kind of help?'

'Light work about the garden. And they'd pay you. All that work they do isn't work at all. They imagine it is. It's just fooling about the garden. What do you say?'

'Whatever you think is best.' He was quite anxious to go to the Sinclairs, drawn to them and, consequently, he was careful not to dampen his father's enthusiasm by showing any of his own.

'Anyhow, we have plenty of time to think about it. I'd say to go. You never know what might come of it if the Sinclairs started to take an interest in you. More people got their start in life that way than by burning the midnight oil.' He could not resist a hit at the late hours the boy studied; 'a woeful waste of fire and light.'

The Sinclairs left for England three days after Christmas, and the Jaguar was absent from Charlie's in the evenings until the first week in March. The night they returned, as the bell above Charlie's door rang out, there was gladness in each, 'They're back!' They had become 'old regulars'. That Saturday Johnny went to the parsonage for the first time.

The jobs were light. He dug, cleared ground, made ridges, wheeled or carried. He had never worked in a garden with anybody before but his father, and by comparison it was a dream working for the Sinclairs. They explained each thing they wanted done clearly, would go over it a second or third time with good humour if he hadn't got it right the first time, always pleased with what had been done well. Though he was uncomfortable at first over the formal lunch, the good hour they spent over a meal, they were so attentive and cheerful that they put him at ease. The hours of the Saturday seemed to fly, were far too short, and often he found himself dreaming of such a life for himself with a woman like Mrs Sinclair in the faraway future when he would grow old.

The wheel of the summer turned pleasantly. The seeds pushed above ground, were thinned. The roses and the other flowers bloomed. The soft fruit ripened and Mrs Sinclair started to make jams in the big brass pot. Each Saturday the boy went home laden with so much fruit and vegetables that he was able to supply Casey's house as well as their own.

Beyond the order and luxury, what he liked best about the house was the silence. There was no idle speech. What words were spoken were direct and towards some definite point. At the barracks, the movement of a fly across the windowpane, Jimmy Farry pushing towards the bridge with his head down, and the cattle cane strapped to the bar of the bicycle, were enough to start an endless flow of conjecture and criticism, especially if Casey was around. 'If you could get close enough to the "huar" you'd hear him counting, counting his cattle and money, counting, counting, counting. . . .'

On one of the more idle Saturdays of the autumn, when they were burning leaves and old stakes and broken branches, the boy felt easy enough with the Colonel to ask him about war and the army.

'The best wars are the wars that are never fought, but for that you need a professional army, so sharp that any possible aggressor would think twice before taking it on. Actual war is a sordid business, but once it begins the army has to do the job as efficiently as possible. It means blowing people's heads off. That's never a pretty business.'

'Did you fight in the front lines?'

'Yes. An officer has to be prepared to go anywhere he sends his men. It is a bad business no matter what civilian nonsense is talked about heroism.' It was plain he had no intention of giving lurid detail and, after a silence asked, 'What do you think you'll do when you enter the big bad world, Johnny?'

'I don't know.'

'You must have some idea of what you'd like to do when you finish school?'

'It depends on what comes up.'

'What do you mean by *what comes up*?'

'Whatever jobs are on offer.'

'Have you ever thought of becoming a soldier – looking for a commission?'

'I'd have no chance of that,' the boy laughed lightly.

'Why not? I thought you were rather good at school, especially at maths.'

'It's not that. I'd have to be a star athlete to stand a chance of a cadetship.'

'For the Irish army?' the Colonel laughed heartily. 'The mile in four minutes.'

'Of course, what other. . . ?'

'There are other armies,' the Colonel was greatly amused. 'What would you say to the British army?'

'That must be even harder still to get into,' the boy answered lightly again, certain that it could never be of any real concern.

'I was trained at Sandhurst. There are some who think it the best military academy in the world. If you were offered a place there, would it interest you?'

'Of course I would be interested.' His own assent seemed far off, so unreal it hardly touched him.

'Would you be interested in a military career?'

'No, not more than any other,' the boy smiled. 'But it'd be more interesting than anything I'd have a chance of here.'

'You know that you could be killed or badly wounded early in life.'

'I know that, but it would be better than working in an office.'

'There's much office work in the military too – but I take it you are interested.'

'Yes Colonel, but you'd have to ask my father. It all depends on what he'd think,' and it occurred to the boy that the father mightn't take to the idea at all. The unreality was sure to end there. The years his father was most proud of were the years of the War of Independence when he was the commander of a small company of men on the run.

The leaves they were burning were catching light, and he went to get the baskets of leaves Mrs Sinclair had left waiting. It was one of the tasks he liked best. When he piled on the leaves he stood back to watch the thick white smoke lift slowly above the beech trees and, as there was no wind, hang like clouds in the dead air.

That evening the Colonel talked with Mrs Sinclair about the idea of getting a commission for Johnny, and it was decided that the Colonel should go to the headmaster of the school secretly to find out exactly how fitted the boy might be.

The school and monastery had been once a British military barracks, though now it had a rounded ecclesiastical door in the high wall, and what had been the drilling square was now a lawn with a few evergreens, one lilac tree, white lawn blocks, and a concrete path that ran straight from the gate to the monastery door.

As soon as Brother Benedict appeared, they shook hands, introducing themselves; and, when the Colonel explained what had brought him, the Brother showed him into a large dining-room full of mahogany and leather, an array of polished silver on the heavy sideboard.

'He does some work for us on Saturdays. Mrs Sinclair and I are quite impressed with him and would like to help him, if that's possible. We just wondered how able is he. He is the type that doesn't give much away.'

'He's the best student we've had for some years,' Brother Benedict smiled. He was from the south, with a clever, handsome face. He wore rimless steel spectacles which he had the habit of polishing from time to time with a pocket handkerchief kept up his sleeve for that purpose alone, holding the spectacles at full length after polishing, while weighing up a situation or person. When not wearing spectacles he seemed to be always smiling, but there was calculation behind the smile. He had heard about the Colonel's visits to Charlie's and was

curious to meet him. He was very fond of good whiskey himself
and thought it a proper occasion to produce his own. From a large
bunch hanging from his belt he selected a small key, unlocked the
sideboard, took out a bottle of Redbreast, and poured two large
measures. 'So, naturally, we are interested in him too. The old
Sergeant is our problem. He's forever trying to push Johnny into
what he calls "gainful" employment. But for all his quiet, he
shouldn't be underestimated. He's a survivor and far from being
without guile. Like the rest of the country he has a great store of
negative capability. He'd much prefer not to.'

'He certainly seemed positive enough about the army.'

After a second Redbreast, the Colonel left well satisfied and
drove directly to the parsonage.

'The boy is as bright as we suspected,' he told Mrs Sinclair. 'His
headmaster turned out to be quite a remarkable man.'

'In what way?'

'Oh, clever, civilized, decent, very clever, in fact. Sort of man
you'd expect to find high up in the army. He keeps an excellent
whiskey. We mustn't forget to leave him a bottle of Black Bush for
Christmas. They don't seem to live badly at all in there.'

That evening the Sinclairs left for Charlie's a half-hour early.
They did not have to go all the way to the barrack gate. The
Sergeant was digging potatoes inside the line of sycamores.
When he saw the Jaguar stop in the avenue, at once he came up to
the wall, bringing the spade to lean on, a glow of pleasure on his
face at the unexpected break in the evening's work.

'Just digging out the few potatoes,' he said to the Colonel, who
got out of the car. 'A real sign that the old year is almost done.'

'Very good ones they seem to be too,' the Colonel responded,
and at once began his proposition.

At first, the Sergeant listened smiling. Obscurely, he had
always felt that some benefit would flow from the association
with the Sinclairs. Soon it grew clear that what was being proposed was no benefit at all. He was not a man to look in any
abstraction on the sparrow's fall. If that small disturbance of the
air was to earn a moment's attention, he would want to know at
once what effect it would have on him or that larger version of
himself that he was fond of referring to as 'my family'. By the time
the Colonel had finished he was speechless with rage.

'It'd mean he'd come out of all that as a British army officer?'

'Precisely. That is, of course, if he is accepted, and proves satisfactory.'

'He couldn't.' He was so choked with emotion that he was barely able to get out the words.

'He seemed to have no objection to the idea.'

'He can't. That's the end of it,' he almost shouted.

'Very well, then. I'm sorry to have disturbed you. Goodbye, Sergeant.'

The Sergeant didn't know what to do with his rage as he watched the black car back out the avenue, turn and snake round by the bridge to Charlie's. He did not move till the post office shut the car from sight, and then, mouthing curses, started to beat the sides of ridges with the spade, only stopping when he felt the handle crack, realizing that he could be seen by someone passing the road. There was no one passing on the road, but even if there were he could always pretend that it was a rat he had been pursuing among the furrows.

The Sergeant waited until the barrack orderly came back on duty and the dayroom door shut again before he went in search of the boy.

'I hear we're about to have a young Sassenach on our hands, an officer and gentleman to boot, not just the usual fool of an Irishman who rushes to the railway station at the first news of a war,' he opened.

'It was Colonel Sinclair who brought it up. I told him he'd have to ask you.'

'And I'm told you're favourably inclined to the idea.'

'I said you'd have to be asked first.'

'Well, then. I have news for you. You're going to no Sandhurst whether they'd have you or not, and I even doubt if the Empire is that hard up. And you're not going to the Sinclairs' this Saturday or any other Saturday, for that matter. I was a fool to countenance the idea in the first place. Well, what do you have to say for yourself?'

'I say that I'm not going,' the boy said, barely able to speak with disappointment and anger.

'And you can say it again if you want,' and the father left him, well satisfied with the damaging restraint of his performance, his self-esteem completely restored.

The following Saturday the Sinclairs lingered a long time over breakfast but at ten-thirty the Colonel rose. 'He's not coming. He was always punctual. He's been stopped.'

'There's a chance he may be ill,' Mrs Sinclair said.

'That would be too much of a coincidence.'

They prepared as usual for the garden, but neither had heart for their separate tasks. They found themselves straying into one another's company, until Mrs Sinclair smiled sadly and said what they had been avoiding. 'It's a hurt.'

'Yes. It is.'

'That's the trouble. We can't help but get attached,' she added quietly. It was the end of no world, they had been through too much for that, but these small hurts seemed to gather with the hurts that had gone before to form a weight that was dispiriting; and, with the perfect tact that is a kind of mind-reading, she said, 'Why don't we forget the garden? I know we have a rule against drinking during the day, but I think we can make an exception today. I promise to try to make an especially nice lunch.'

'What kind of wine?' he asked.

'Red wine,' she said at once.

'I suppose the lesson is that we should have let well enough alone,' he said.

'I had my doubts all along but I suppose I was hoping they weren't true. I don't really think that we'd have arranged to get him into Sandhurst in the first place; but if we had, his trouble would have just begun – his whole background, his accent most of all. It's hopeless to even contemplate. Let's make lunch.'

The boy hung about the gravel outside the barracks that morning. Casey was the barrack orderly again. All the others were out on patrol. After he had finished the *Independent*, Casey came out to join the boy on the gravel.

'This must be the first Saturday in a long time you aren't away helping the Colonel,' Guard Casey probed gently.

'I was stopped,' he replied with open bitterness.

'I suppose it'll be the end of the free fruit and vegetables. I hear they were threatening to make a British officer out of you.'

'I wouldn't have minded. Many go from here to England to work.'

'Your father would never have been able to live with that. You

really have to be born into that class of people. You don't ever
find robins feeding with the sparrows.'

'Will the Sergeant be out on evening patrol?'

'I'll have a look.'

Johnny followed Casey over the hollow, scrubbed boards of
the dayroom, where the policeman looked in the big ledger.

'He is. From six to nine. In the Crossna direction.'

It was in the opposite direction to the Colonel's. During those
hours he would go to the parsonage to explain why he had not
come to them, how it had ended.

Just after six, as soon as the Sergeant was out of sight, the boy
crossed the bridge with a hazel fishing rod. Though it was too
late for the small fish, perch or roach, he could say he was
throwing a line out as a sort of experiment, for fun; but as soon
as he was across the bridge he hid it behind a wall and took to
the fields. Running, walking, running, scrambling across the
stone walls, keeping well away from the farmhouses, he was
soon close to the parsonage, which he circled, coming up
through the orchard at the back. He was so mindless with the
fear of not getting to the house in secret that he could hardly
remember why he had set out, when he found himself at the
kitchen window looking in at the Colonel and Mrs Sinclair
seated at the big table with wine glasses in their hands. They
were so absorbed in their conversation that he had to tap the
window before they noticed. They both rose to let him in.

'It wasn't my fault, I would have come today as usual if he'd
let me.' Hard as he tried, he wasn't able to beat down a sudden
attack of sobbing. They allowed him to quiet and Mrs Sinclair
got him a large glass of raspberry cordial.

'Of course it wasn't your fault. That's the very last thing
anybody could imagine,' Mrs Sinclair put the glass in his hand,
gently touching his hair.

'In fact, it was all our fault. Our proposal upset everything,'
Colonel Sinclair said. 'We didn't think it through.' He didn't
know what to give the boy, knew he wouldn't accept money
and, in a fit of weary inspiration, he went upstairs to fetch a
book on natural history that had been their son's favourite book
when young. He first checked with his wife, and when she
nodded he gave it to the boy. 'It's something we want you to
have. We intended to give it to you for Christmas.'

In spite of the gift, he knew that it was all closing down. With kindness but with firmness, the Sinclairs were now more separate than the evening the Colonel had come to the barracks with the basket of apples. A world had opened that evening; it was closing now like curtains being silently drawn, and all the more finally because there was not even a shadow of violence.

It had not been easy to face the Sinclairs. He had made clear his own position, and he felt freed. When he got to the bridge, he took the hazel rod from beneath the wall and held it in full view, hiding the book under his coat. He met no one. There were no bicycles against the barrack wall. The policemen hadn't come in off patrol. He was about to drop in on Casey when he noticed that there was already someone there, a tall young man who was standing in his bare feet against the wall beneath the measuring bar, which Casey was adjusting.

'You're the height, all right. A good five-eleven and a half. Now lift your arms till we find out if you have the chest measurements as well.'

'I've them, all right, Guard Casey,' the young man laughed nervously, 'But what I'm most afraid of is the Irish.'

'You needn't be a bit afeard. I'm one of the few guards fluent in two languages, the best *Rosses Blas* from the cradle, and I haven't a quarter use for even one language, so don't you worry about the Irish.'

The weak sun was going down beyond Oakport Wood. Only the muscling river moved. In another hour the Sinclairs' car would be crossing the bridge to Charlie's. An hour after that the Sergeant would come in off patrol. That seemed the whole endless world then.

The burning of Rockingham House stood out from all else in the still-emptying countryside in the next few years. In that amazing night all was lit up, the whole lake and its islands all the way across to the Rockadoon and first slopes of the Curlews, the great beech walk going towards Boyle, the woods behind the house, and over them the High Plains, the light leaping even to Greatmeadow. The glass of the three hundred and sixty-five windows shattered. The roof came down. Among the priceless things said to have been lost was a rocking chair that could be drawn as a sleigh, beautifully carved leopards asleep on the armrests, one of three made by the great German craftsmen of St Petersburg for Catherine the Great. All that remained of the front of the house overlooking the lake and islands was the magnificent shell and portals, now full of sky and dangerous in high winds. Only rooms in the servants' quarters in the part of the basement next to the sunken tennis courts had escaped the fire. Sir Cecil and Lady King-Harmon, who had been much photographed during the week at the Newmarket Yearling Sales, came home at once, and took over a floor of the Royal Hotel.

Talk ran riot. All small suspicious burnings usual to the area were forgotten about: ramshackle farmhouses soaked in paraffin, a candle lit in a tin container above saturated rags and wood, doors and windows secured, the owners off to town for the day. During the six hours it would take the candle to burn down, they'd make sure to be seen in every shop and pub in town, and come home in darkness to find the house blazing in a bright promise of insurance money.

No house had been insured more handsomely than the great house built by Nash above Lough Key. Suspicion and old caste hostility scenting power in the turning of the wheel was enough to rouse the Sergeant to covert but vigorous investigation. There had been carelessness. A house steward under suspicion in a number of cases of arson in Canada had been hired just six weeks before. A wild drunken party had been held in the servants' quarters the night before the fire, champagne and rare brandies drunk. There had been loose talk. The Sergeant filed all this as preliminary evidence and asked permission to begin formal inquiries. He was warned off at once. Sir Cecil was one of the Councillors of State. When the Sergeant obstinately persisted, he was given notice of transfer to Donegal. This he countered by resigning. He had reached the age when he was entitled to retire on reduced pension. A twelve-acre farm that had once been the nursery farm for the gardens of Rockingham, with a stone house, the traditional residence of the head gardener of Rockingham, came on the market. He bought it and left the barracks. It stood just outside the Demesne Wall, a small iron gate in the wall, and a bridle path led from it to Rockingham House. It was said to have been used by the different ladies of Rockingham when they came to choose plants for the house

gardens. The surprisingly exotic plants from as far away as
China and India that grew wild here and there on the farm
meant nothing to the Sergeant. He bought cows and a tractor,
began to send milk to the creamery, put down a potato patch,
fought a losing battle each harvest with the pigeons from the
estate woods over his rood of oats. It was an exact replica of the
life he'd lived as a boy.

A small ceremony in the rose garden of the parsonage at
Ardcarne that year would have passed unnoticed even if there
had been no great fire. Mrs Sinclair had died in a London clinic
after a long illness. She had asked for her ashes to be scattered in
the rose garden of 'the dear house'. The Colonel, his daughter,
son-in-law, and two grandchildren brought the ashes from
London. On a wet, windy afternoon the daughter released the
ashes from the urn. She did it nervously and some of the dust
blew back in her face, sticking to her hair and clothes. They all
stayed in the Royal that night, and the next day the young
family left for Durham.

The Colonel opened the house as soon as they'd gone. But he
did not go to Charlie's that evening. Instead, he went to the
Royal, and this he continued to do as regularly as once Mrs
Sinclair and he had set out for Charlie's. The Rockingham
woods were sold. Sawmills were set up, and to everybody's
surprise the Colonel became manager of McAinish's Mill. To
begin with, he was unpopular with the workmen, insisting on
strict timekeeping, which was in opposition to the casual local
sense of coming and going, fining each man an hour's pay for
every fifteen minutes late; but he was fair, and it was said that
he came to know as much about the saws and machinery as any
mechanic in the woods, and it became the best and happiest of
the mills. Though he always remained aloof, there grew an
unspoken loyalty between him and his men.

Colonel Sinclair bought a small turkey in Boyle that Christmas
Eve. It was all he needed for the holiday. There was fruit in the
house, wine, a few heads of lettuce still in the greenhouse. Then
he went for a stroll in the streets. Mrs Sinclair had been very
fond of this town. It was a bright, clear night, brighter still with
the strings of Christmas lights climbing towards the star above
the clock on the Crescent. *Gerald Dodd, Town Commissioner* had
gone to join the Rockinghams on the clock's memorial stone.

The Colonel approved but it also made him smile. Surrounded on the stone by the formidable roll call of Staffords and King-Harmons the name Gerald Dodd had the effect of a charming and innocent effrontery. The King-Harmons would certainly not have approved. The Staffords would have been outraged. On the other side of the river the broken roof of the old British military barracks was white with frost. From one chimneypiece an elder grew. Amid it all the shallow river raced beneath the gentle curve of the bridge, rushed past the white walls of the Royal on its way out towards Key. About him people clapped one another on backs and shoulders. The air was thickly warm with Happy Christmases. The Colonel walked very slowly, enjoying the crowd but feeling outside the excitement. He shook hands affably with a few neighbours, touched his cap to the women, wishing them a Merry Christmas. He shook hands with men who worked for him in the mill, but he neither offered drinks nor was he asked.

In the Royal, he caught the page boy in the mirror making faces behind his back as he took off his old Burberry, but he did not mind. He was old and the page boy could do without his tip. He sat alone at one of the river windows and ordered smoked salmon with brown bread and a half-bottle of white wine.

When he did not appear at the mill the first morning after the holiday, the foreman and one of the men went to the parsonage. The key was in the front door, but there was no answer to their knocking. They found him just inside the door, at the foot of the stairs. In the kitchen two places were laid at the head of the big table. There was a pair of napkins in silver rings and two wine glasses beside the usual cutlery. A small turkey lay in an ovenware dish beside the stove, larded and stuffed, ready for roasting. An unwashed wilting head of lettuce stood on the running board of the sink.

As an announcement of a wedding or pregnancy after a lull seems to provoke a sudden increase in such activities, so it happened with the Sergeant's early retirement from the force. The first to follow was Guard Casey. He had no interest in land and used his gratuity to pay the deposit on a house in Sligo. There he got a job as the yard-man in a small bakery, and years of intense happiness began. His alertness, natural kindness, interest in everything that went on around him, made him instantly loved. What wasn't noticed at first was his insatiable thirst for news. Some of the bread vans went as far as the barracks, and it seemed natural enough that he should be interested in places and people he had served most of his life. In fact, these van men took his interest as a form of flattery, lifting for a few moments their sense of the daily dullness of their round; but then it was noticed that he was almost equally interested in people he had never met, places he had never been to. In a comparatively short time he had acquired a detailed knowledge of all the van routes and the characters of the more colourful shopkeepers, even of some who had little colour.

'A pure child. No wit. Mad for news,' was the way the passion was affectionately indulged. 'He should be fed lots. Tell him plenty of lies.' But he seemed to have an unerring sense as to what was fact and what was malicious invention.

'Sunday is so long. It's so hard to put in.'

Guard Casey kept the walk and air of a young man well into his seventies and went on working at the bakery. It was a simple fall crossing the yard to open the gates one wet morning that heralded an end, a broken hip that would not heal. He and his family had grown unused to one another over the years. They now found each other's company burdensome, and it was to his relief as well as theirs when it was agreed that he would get better care in the regional hospital when it was clear that he wasn't going to get well, as everything but his spirit was sinking. Then his family, through their religious connections, found a bed for him in St Joseph's Hospice of the Dying in Dublin. It was there he was visited by the Sergeant's son, who had heard that he missed company.

'They're nearly all gone now anyhow, God have mercy on them. *Is me Oisín i ndiadh na feinne*,' he laughed.

'Wouldn't you think when they're so full of religion that they'd have shifted themselves this far to see you?' It was open criticism of his family.

'No, not at all. It's too far.' He lifted his hand as if to clear the harshness which seemed to take on an unpleasant moral note in the face of this largeness of spirit. 'No one in their right mind travels so far to follow losing teams. And this is a losing team,' he started to laugh again but was forced to stop because of coughing. 'Still, I've known the whole world,' he said when he recovered.

Johnny justified Brother Benedict's account of his ability to Colonel Sinclair by winning a scholarship to university the following year.

'You'll be like the rest of the country – educated away beyond your intelligence,' was the father's unenthusiastic response, and they saw very little of one another over the next few years. The boy spent the vacations in England, working on building sites and in canning factories around London. A good primary degree allowed him to baffle his father even further by continuing postgraduate study in psychology, and he was given a lectureship in the university when he completed his doctorate. Then he obtained work with the new television station, first in an advisory role, but later he made a series of documentary films about the darker aspects of Irish life. As they were controversial, they won him a sort of fame: some thought they were serious, well made, and compulsive viewing, bringing things to light that were in bad need of light; but others maintained that they were humourless, morbid, and restricted to a narrow view that was more revealing of private obsessions than any truths about life or Irish life in general. During this time he made a few attempts to get on with his father, but it was more useless than ever.

'There have to be rules if there's to be any fairness or freedom,' he argued the last time they met.

'What if we don't feel like dancing to those rules of yours?'

'They're not my rules.'

'One thing sure is that they're not mine either. So what'll you do?'

'I just won't see you.'

'I don't think that will kill me.'

The tide that emptied the countryside more than any other since the famine has turned. Hardly anybody now goes to England. Some who went came home to claim inheritances, and stayed, old men waiting at the ends of lanes on Sunday evenings for the minibus to take them to church bingo. Most houses have a car and colour television. The bicycles and horses, carts and traps and sidecars, have gone from the roads. A big yellow bus brings the budding scholars to school in the town, and it is no longer uncommon to go on to university. The mail car is orange. Just one policeman with a squad car lives in the barracks.

The tide that had gone out to America and every part of
Britain now reaches only as far as a bursting Dublin, and every
Friday night crammed buses take the aliens home. For a few free
days in country light they feel important until the same buses
take them back on Sunday night to shared flats and bed-sits.
Storage heaters have been installed in the church in the village.
The damp did not leave the limestone. The dark evergreens
shutting out the light were blamed and cut down, revealing the
church in all its huge, astonishing ugliness amid the headstones
of former priests of the parish inside the low wall that marked
off a corner of Henry's field. The damp still did not leave the
limestone, but in spite of it the church is full to overflowing
every Sunday.

As in other churches, the priest now faces the people,
acknowledging that they are the mystery. He is a young priest
and tells them that God is on their side and wants them to want
children, bungalow bliss, a car, and colour television. Heaven is
all about us, hell is in ourselves and in one moment can be
exorcized. Many of the congregation chat with one another and
read newspapers all through the Sacrifice. The words are in
English and understandable. The congregation gives out the
responses. The altar boys kneeling in scarlet and white at the
foot of the altar steps ring the bell and attend the priest, but they
no longer have to learn Latin.

No one beats a path to the presbytery. The young priest is
seldom there and has no housekeeper. Nights, when he's not
supervising church bingo, he plays the guitar and sings at local
hotels where he is a hit with tourists. He seldom wears black or
the Roman collar. To show how little it means to him, one
convivial evening in a hotel at Lough Arrow he pulled the collar
from his neck and dropped it into the soup. When the piece of
white plastic was fished out amid the laughter, it was found to
have been made in Japan.

A politician lives outside the village, and the crowd that once
flocked to the presbytery now go to him instead. Certain nights
he holds 'clinics'. They are advertised. On 'clinic' nights a line of
cars can be seen standing for several hundred yards along the
road past his house, the car radios playing. On cold nights the
engines run. No one thinks it wasteful anymore. They come to
look for grants, to try to get drunken driving convictions

squashed, to get free medical cards, sickness benefit, to have
planning application decisions that have gone against them
reversed, to get children into jobs. As they all have votes they are
never 'run'.

The Protestants have all gone, but the church in Ardcarne is
still opened once a year. No one attends it now. There was a move
to have the famous Purser windows taken out and installed in a
new church being built in the North of Ireland. This was preven-
ted by the conditions of the endowment. They have not been
vandalized.

Sir Cecil and Lady King-Harmon bought a stud farm outside
Dublin. The Land Commission took over the estate and split it
into farms, preserving the gardens and woods and walks immediately around the house as a forest park. The roofless shell of the
Chapel-of-Ease stands by the boathouse. Within, lovers scratch
their names on the stone. Pleasure craft ply the lake and its
islands with day trippers all through the summer. The tall Nash
shell stood for a few years above the lake until it was condemned
as dangerous, and dynamited. A grey concrete lookout tower,
looking cold and wet even in the sun, was built in its place.

In every house across the countryside there glows at night the
strange living light of television sets, more widespread than the
little red lamps before the pictures of the Sacred Heart years
before.

The Sergeant's son came with a television crew to make a film
for a series called *My Own Place*. He was older than when his
father first came to the barracks. The crew put up in the Royal,
and the priest was invited to dinner the first night to counter any
hostility they might have run into while filming. It showed how
out of touch the producer was with the place. He should have
invited the politician.

The light was good the next morning, and they decided to
begin filming at the old Georgian parsonage in Ardcarne. They
hoped to go from there to the Protestant church and the burial
place of the King-Harmons, and then to the village if the light
held. They would be doing well if they got through all that in one
day. They set up the cameras and microphones under the beech
trees on the avenue where once he had happily burned leaves for
the Sinclairs. It would be a dull film. There would be no people in
it. The people that interested him were all dead.

'Take two, cut one,' the clapboard was brought down and the continuity girl lifted her stopwatch. The Sergeant's son started walking slowly down the grass-grown avenue into the camera.

'After the war, Colonel Sinclair and his wife came home from London to this parsonage. His father had been the parson here. It must have looked much as it looks now when they first came. They restored it, house and garden and orchard and paddocks and lawn. I think they were very happy here, but now all is wilderness again.'

The camera panned slowly away from the narrator to the house, and continued along the railings that had long lost their second whiteness, whirring steadily in the silence as it took in only what was in front of it, despite the cunning hand of the cameraman: lingering on the bright rain of cherries on the tramped grass beneath the trees, the flaked white paint of the paddock railing, the Iron Mountains smoky and blue as they stretched into the North against the rim of the sky.

Like All Other Men

He watched her for a long time among the women across the dancefloor in the half-light of the afternoon. She wasn't tall or beautiful, but he couldn't take his eyes away. Some of the women winced palpably and fell back as they were passed over. Others stood their ground and stared defiantly back. She seemed quietly indifferent, taking a few steps back into the thinning crowd each time she found herself isolated on the floor. When she was asked to dance, she behaved exactly the same. She flashed no smile, gave no giddy shrug of triumph to betray the tension of the wait, the redeemed vanity.

Nurses, students, actors and actresses, musicians, some prostitutes, people who worked in restaurants and newspapers, nightwatchmen, a medley of the old and very young, came to these afternoon dances. Michael Duggan came every Saturday and Sunday. He was a teacher of Latin and history in a midlands town forty miles from Dublin, and each Friday he came in on the evening bus to spend the whole weekend round the cinemas and restaurants and dancehalls of O'Connell Street. A year before he had been within a couple of months of ordination.

When he did cross to ask her to dance, she followed him with the same unconcern on to the floor as she had showed just standing there. She danced beautifully, with a strong, easy freedom. She was a nurse in the Blanchardstown Chest Hospital. She came from Kerry. Her father was a National Teacher near Killarney. She had been to these afternoon dances before, but not for a couple of years. Her name was Susan Spillane.

'I suppose everybody asks you these questions,' he said.

'The last one did anyhow,' she smiled. 'You'd better tell me about yourself as well.' She had close curly black hair, an intelligent face, and there was something strange about her eyes.

'Are your eyes two different colours?'

'One eye is brown, the other grey. I may have got the grey eye by mistake. All the others in the house have brown eyes.'

'They are lovely.' The dance had ended. He had let her go. It was not easy to thread a way through these inanities of speech.

A girl could often stand unnoticed a long time, and then it was enough for one man to show an interest to start a rush. When the next two dances were called, though he moved quickly each time, he was beaten to her side. The third dance was a ladies' choice, and he withdrew back into the crowd of men. She followed him into the crowd, and this time he did not let her slip away when the dance ended. It was a polite convention for women to make a show of surprise when invited for a drink, of having difficulty making up their minds, but she said at once she'd love a drink, and asked for whiskey.

'I hardly drink at all, but I like the burnt taste,' and she sipped the small measure neat for the two hours that were left of the dance. 'My father loves a glass of whiskey late at night. I've often sat and had a sip with him.'

They danced again and afterwards came back to the table, sipped the drinks, sat and talked, and danced again. Time raced.

'Do you have to go on night duty tonight?' he asked as it moved near the time when the band would stand and play the anthem. He was afraid he would lose her then.

'No. I'm on tomorrow night.'

'Maybe you'd eat something with me this evening?'

'I'd like that.'

There was still some daylight left when they came from the dancehall, and they turned away from it into a bar. They both had coffee. An hour later, when he knew it was dark outside, he asked awkwardly, 'I suppose it's a bit outrageous to suggest a walk before we look for a place to eat,' his guilty smile apologizing for such a poor and plain admission of the sexual.

'I don't see why not.' She smiled. 'I'd like a walk.'

'What if it's raining?' He gave them both the excuse to draw back.

'There's only one way to find out,' she said.

It was raining very lightly, the street black and shining under the lamps, but she didn't seem to mind the rain, nor that the walk led towards the dark shabby streets west of O'Connell

Street. There they found a dark doorway and embraced. She returned his kisses with the same directness and freedom with which she had danced, but people kept continually passing in the early evening dark, until they seemed to break off together to say, 'This is useless,' and arm in arm to head back towards the light.

'It's a pity we haven't some room or place of our own,' he said.

'Where did you spend last night?' she asked.

'Where I stay every weekend, a rooming house in North Earl Street, four beds to the room. It'd be no place to go.'

It was no place to go. A dumb man in the next bed to his had been very nearly beaten up the night before. The men who took the last two beds had been drinking. They woke the dumb man while they fumbled for the light, and he sat up in his bed and gestured towards the partly open window as soon as the light came on. Twice he made the same upward movement with his thumb: he wanted them to try to close the window because of the cold wind blowing in. The smaller of the two men misinterpreted the gesture and with a shout fell on the man. They realized that he was dumb when he started to squeal. She didn't laugh at the story.

'It's not hard to give the wrong signals in this world.'

'We could go to a hotel,' she said. He was stopped dead in his tracks. 'That's if you want to, and only – only – if I can pay half.'

'What hotel?'

'Are you certain you'd want that? It doesn't matter to me,' she was looking into his face.

'There's nothing I want more in the world, but where?' He stood between desire and fear.

'The Clarence across the river is comfortable and fairly inexpensive.'

'Will we see if we can get a room before we eat or afterwards?' He was clumsy with diffidence in the face of what she had proposed.

'We might as well look now, but are you certain?'

'I'm certain. And you?'

'As long as you agree that I can pay half,' she said.

'I agree.'

They sealed one another's lips and crossed the river by the Halfpenny Bridge.

'Do you think we will have any trouble?' he asked as they drew close to the hotel.

'We'll soon find out. I think we both look respectable enough,' and for the first time he thought he felt some nervousness in her handclasp, and it made him feel a little easier.

There was no trouble. They were given a room with a bath on the second floor.

'I liked it very much that you gave your real name,' she said when they were alone.

'Why?'

'It seemed more open, honest. . . .'

'It was the only name I could think of at the time.'

'I still like it,' she said, and their nervousness found release in laughter.

The bathroom was just inside the door. The bed and bedside lamp and table were by the window, a chair and writing table in the opposite corner, two armchairs in the middle of the room. The window looked down on the night city and the river. He drew the curtains and took her in his arms.

'Wait,' she said. 'We've plenty of time before going out to eat.'

While she was in the bathroom he turned off the light, slipped from his clothes, and got into the bed to wait for her.

'Why did you turn out the light?' she asked sharply when she came from the bathroom.

'I thought you'd want it out.'

'I want to see what I'm doing.'

It was not clear whether she wanted the light for the practical acts of undressing or that she wanted these preliminaries to what is called the act of darkness to be free of all furtiveness, that they should be noted with care like the names of places passed on an important journey.

'I'm sorry,' he said, and turned on the bedside lamp. He watched her slow, sure movements as she stepped from her clothes, how strong and confident and beautiful she was. 'Do you still want the light on?' he asked as she came towards him.

'No.'

'You are beautiful.' He wanted to say that her naked beauty took his breath away, was almost hurtful.

What he had wanted so much that it had become frightening she made easy, but it was almost impossible to believe that he now rested in the still centre of what had long been a dream. After long deprivation the plain pleasures of bed and table grow sadly mystical.

'Have you slept with anyone before?' he asked.

'Yes, with one person.'

'Were you in love with him?'

'Yes.'

'Are you still in love with him?'

'No. Not at all.'

'I never have.'

'I know.'

They came again into one another's arms. There was such peace afterwards that the harsh shrieking of the gulls outside, the even swish of the traffic along the quays was but more part of that peace.

Is this all? Common greed and restlessness rose easily to despise what was so hard come by as soon as it was gained, so luckily, so openly given. But before that had any time to grow there was the grace of dressing, of going out to eat together in the surety that they were coming back to this closed room. He felt like a young husband, as he waited for her to finish dressing.

The light drizzle of the early evening had turned into a downpour by the time they came down, the hotel lobby crowded with people in raincoats, many carrying umbrellas.

'We're guaranteed a drowning if we head out in that.'

'We don't need to. We can eat here. The grill is open.'

It was a large, very pleasant room with light wood panelling and an open fire at its end. She picked the lamb cutlets, he the charcoaled steak, and they each had a glass of red wine.

'This has to be split evenly as well,' she said.

'I don't see why. I'd like to take you.'

'That was the bargain. It must be kept,' she smiled. 'How long have you been teaching?'

'Less than a year. I was in Maynooth for a long time.'

'Were you studying for the priesthood?'

'That's what people mostly do there,' he said drily. 'I left with only a couple of months to go. It must sound quite bad.'

'It's better than leaving afterwards. Why did you leave?' she asked with formidable seriousness. It could not be turned aside with sarcasm or even irony.

'Because I no longer believed. I could hardly lead others to a life that I didn't believe in myself. When I entered Maynooth at eighteen I thought the whole course of my life was settled. It wasn't.'

'There must be something,' she insisted.

'There may well be, but I don't know what it is.'

'Was it because you needed . . . to be married?'

'No, not sex,' he said. 'Though that's what many people think. If anything, the giving up of sex – renunciation was the word we used – gave the vocation far more force. We weren't doing anything easy. That has its own pride: we were giving up an idea of pleasure for a far greater good; that is, until belief started to go, and then all went.'

'You don't believe in anything at all, then?' she said with a gravity that both charmed and nettled.

'I have no talent for profundity,' he had spoken more than he had intended and was beginning to be irritated by the turn of the conversation.

'You must believe in something?' she insisted.

'"Tis most certain. Have not the schoolmen said it?' he quoted to tease gently, but saw she disliked the tone. 'I believe in honour, decency, affection, in pleasure. This, for instance, is a very good steak.'

'You don't seem bitter.' This faint praise was harder to take than blame.

'That would be very stupid. That would be worst of all. How is the lamb?'

'It's good, but I don't like to be fobbed off like that.'

'I wouldn't do that. I still find it painful, that's all. I'm far too grateful to you. I think you were very brave to come here,' he started to fumble again, gently, diffidently.

'I wasn't brave. It was what I wanted.'

'Not many women would have the courage to propose an hotel.'

'They might be the wise ones.'

It was her turn to want to change the direction of the conversation. A silence fell that wasn't silence. They were unsure, their minds working furiously behind the silence to find some safe way to turn.

'That man you were in love with,' he suggested.

'He was married. He had a son. He travelled in pharmaceuticals.'

'That doesn't sound too good for you.'

'It wasn't. It was a mess.'

They had taken another wrong turning.

It was still pouring when they came from the grill. They had one very slow drink in the hotel bar, watching the people drink and come and go before the room and night drew them.

In the morning he asked, 'What are you doing today?'

'I'll go back to the hospital, probably try to get some sleep. I'm on night duty at eight.'

'We didn't get much sleep last night.'

'No, we didn't,' she answered gently enough, but making it plain that she had no interest in the reference. 'What are you doing?' she changed the subject.

'There are three buses back. I'll have to get one of them.'

'Which one?'

'Probably the twelve o'clock, since you're going back to the hospital. When will we meet again?' he asked in a tone that already took the meeting for granted.

She was half-dressed. The vague shape of her thighs shone through the pale slip as she turned towards him. 'We can't meet again.'

'Why not?' The casualness changed. 'Is there something wrong?'

'Nothing. Nothing at all. The very opposite.'

'What's the matter, then? Why can't we meet?'

'I was going to tell you last night and didn't. I thought it might spoil everything. After all, you were in Maynooth once. I'm joining an Order.'

'You must be joking.'

'I was never more serious in my life. I'm joining next Thursday . . . the Medical Missionaries.' She had about her that presence that had attracted him in the dancehall; she stood free of everything around her, secure in her own light.

'I can't believe you.'

'It's true,' she said.

'But the whole thing is a lie, a waste, a fabrication.'

'It's not for me and it wasn't once for you.'

'But I believed then.'

'Don't you think I do?' she said sharply.

'To mouth Hail Marys and Our Fathers all of your life.'

'You know that's cheap. It'll be mostly work. I'll nurse as I nurse now. In two years' time I'll probably be sent to medical school. The Order has a great need of its own doctors.'

'Wasn't last night a strange preparation for your new life?'

'I don't see much wrong with it.'

'From your point of view, wasn't it a sin?' he was angry now.

'Not much of a one, if it was. I've known women who spent the night before their marriage with another man. It was an end to their free or single life.'

'And I was the goodbye, the shake-hands?'

'I didn't plan it. I was attracted to you. We were free. That's the way it fell. If I did it after joining, it would be different. It would be a very great sin.'

'Perhaps we could be married?' he pressed blindly.

'No. You wouldn't ask so lightly if we could.'

'We wouldn't have much at first but we would have one another and we could work,' he pursued.

'No. I'm sorry. I like you very much, but it cannot be. My mind has been made up for a long time.'

'Well, one last time then,' he cut her short.

'Hadn't we the whole night?'

'One last time,' his hands insisted: and as soon as it was over he was sorry, left with less than if it had never taken place.

'I'm sorry,' he said.

'It doesn't matter.'

After they had paid downstairs, they did not want to eat in the hotel, though the grill room was serving breakfast. They went to one of the big plastic and chrome places on O'Connell Street. They ate slowly in uneasy silence.

'I hope you'll forgive me, if there's anything to forgive,' she said after a long time.

'I was going to ask the same thing. There's nothing to forgive. I wanted to see you again, to go on seeing you. I never thought I'd have the luck to meet someone so open . . . so unafraid,' he was entangled in his own words before he'd finished.

'I'm not like that at all,' she laughed as she hadn't for a long time. 'I'm a coward. I'm frightened of next week. I'm frightened by most things.'

'Why don't you take an address that'll always find me in case you change your mind?'

'I'll not change.'

'I thought that once too.'

'No. I'll not. I can't,' she said, but he still wrote the address and slipped it in her pocket.

'You can throw it away as soon as I'm out of sight.'

As they rose he saw that her eyes were filled with tears.

They now leaned completely on those small acts of ceremony that help us better out of life than any drug. He paid at the cash desk and waited afterwards while she fixed her scarf, smiled ruefully as he stood aside to allow her the inside of the stairs, opened the large swing-door at the bottom of the steps. They walked slowly to the bus stop. At the stop they tried to foretell the evening's weather by the dark cloudy appearance of the sky towards the west. The only thing that seemed certain was that there'd be more rain. They shook hands as the bus came in. He waited until all the passengers had got on and it had moved away.

The river out beyond the Custom House, the straight quays, seemed to stretch out in the emptiness after she had gone. In my end is my beginning, he recalled well. In my beginning is my end, his and hers, mine and thine. It seemed to stretch out as complete as the emptiness, as endless as a wedding ring. He knew it like his own breathing. There might well be nothing, but she was still prepared to live by that one thing, to will it true.

Thinking of her, he found himself walking eagerly towards the Busarus. But he knew that no matter how eagerly he found himself walking in any direction now it could only take him to the next day, and the next.

Eddie Mac

The summer Annie May Moran came to work for Mrs Kirkwood was the great year of St Michael's football. The team had reached the Final of the Senior Cup for the second year running. Eddie Mac was their star, their finest forward. He worked for the Kirkwoods and lived in the three-roomed herdsman's cottage at the end of the yard, its galvanized roof sprayed the same shade of green as the stables. The two Kirkwoods, father and son, old William and young Master William, went to Roscommon to watch the final. They barely understood the game and were not touched by the wild fever that emptied the countryside on that late August Sunday: 'We went because Eddie was playing. His father would have enjoyed this day, had he stayed.'

Annie May helped Mrs Kirkwood set the dinner table in the front room that afternoon while the game was being played. Mrs Kirkwood went to particular care with the linen and silver, and the best set of bone china was on display. The Nutleys of Oakport, the oldest and last of her local friends, were coming to dinner that evening. When she was satisfied with the arrangement of the room and had checked the food, she took her book and sat in the rocking chair in the library, where, looking out on the lawn and white paling and the winding avenue of copper and green beech, she rocked herself to sleep as she did every day at this hour.

Exploding cans of carbide, random shouts and cheers and whistles as fires were lit on the hills and on every cross on the roadways woke her early. St Michael's had won the Senior Cup for the first time since its founding. She rose and came down to Annie May in the kitchen. 'It's an unmitigated disaster,' she confided to the servant girl. 'It was bad enough last year, and they lost. What'll it be like now that they have won?'

'Eddie was the hero,' William Kirkwood announced when they returned from Roscommon. 'The two goals he scored in the second half won the game – it broke the other team's heart. They carried him on their shoulders all around the field with the cup at the end.' Annie May coloured as he spoke. She was already in love with the young herdsman who had yet to acknowledge her presence in the house.

A week later, the big silver cup arrived in Kirkwood's yard on its round of the parish, the red and green ribbons streaming from the handles. Again Eddie Mac was hoisted on shoulders and carried aloft with the cup to his own door. Inside the small house the cup was filled to the brim with whiskey. Cheers rang out as each person drank from the cup. A large bonfire was set ablaze in the middle of the yard. A melodeon started to play.

'It's so childish,' Mrs Kirkwood complained in the big house. 'We can abandon any hope of sleep tonight.'

'They're entitled to the night,' her husband argued. 'It's a pity Eddie's father isn't around. He would have greatly enjoyed the night. They've had a famous victory.'

'And they use it to get drunk! Is that a way to celebrate decently? Listen to that din down in the yard.'

'I think you are too hard on them, Elisabeth,' William Kirkwood countered gently.

At that time, Annie May was too young to go to the dances and Eddie Mac had not yet the reputation of a womanizer. He went with the one girl, Kathleen Duignan. She was tall and dark and they looked like brother and sister. As the Duignans owned land, they were a class above the Macs, and when Kathleen Duignan went to England at Christmas it was thought she had thrown Eddie over. He was never to go with another girl for so long.

A few months later, a torn knee in spring training was to end his football glory. Without him the team struggled through the early rounds of the championship, and when he returned for the semi-final he played poorly. The injury did not affect his walk but showed as soon as he tried to sprint or leap. His whole game was based on speed and anticipation. He had neither taste nor appetite for the rough and tumble. Now that his deadly grace was gone, his style of hanging back till the last moment looked like cowardice. As soon as it was plain that the cup was about to be lost, Eddie was taunted and jeered every time he went near the ball by the same people that had chaired him shoulder high from the field the year before. On the surface he showed no feeling, and walked stonefaced from the field; but on the following Wednesday, the evening every week he walked to the village to collect his copy of the *Herald* and to buy in a few groceries, he put his studded boots, football socks, togs, bandages in his green and red jersey, and by drawing the sleeves round and knotting them tightly made it a secure bundle, which he dropped in the deepest arch as he crossed the bridge into the village, only waiting long enough after the splash to be certain it had sunk.

A gentle and even more final end came that September to Mrs Kirkwood. She had gone with her book to sit in the rocking chair in front of the library window 'in the one hour of the day selfishly my own'. When she did not come down to the kitchen at her usual time, Annie May waited for half an hour before going up to the front room. The chair was still imperceptibly rocking before the window, but the book had fallen, and when she called there was no answer. An intense stillness was in the room. Even the spaces between the beech trees down the rich avenue seemed to gaze back in their emptiness, and she ran shouting for help to the yard.

The formal heart of the house, perhaps the heart of the house itself, stopped with Mrs Kirkwood. William Kirkwood and his son seemed only too glad not to have to go out to dinner anymore, and they no longer received people at the house. They took all their meals in the big kitchen and did not dress up even on Sunday. Old William's sole interest in years had been his bees. Now he was able to devote himself to them exclusively; and his son, who had lost money introducing a new strain of Cheviots to the farm and running it according to the tenets of his agricultural college, let it fall back into Eddie Mac's hands, who ran it on the traditional lines of his father before him, not making money but losing none. All Master William's time now turned back to a boyhood fascination with astronomy, and he pursued the stars with much the same gentle, singular dedication as his father accorded the bees, ordering books and instruments, entering into correspondence with other amateur astronomers. He spent most clear nights out in the fields examining the stars through a long telescope fixed on a tripod.

Freed from Mrs Kirkwood's disapproval of all that went on in
the village, Annie May was now able to go to the dances. She
was large and plain but had her admirers, young men off
farms – and some young no longer, but without any sense of
their ageing, who judged cattle from the rear and preferred a
good armful to any lustre of eye or line of cheekbone or throat.
Her eyes were still only for Eddie Mac, but he did not even smile
or nod to her in the hall. She would see him standing among the
other men at the back of the hall, lazily smoking as his eyes went
over the girls that danced past. Sometimes he just stood there
for the whole night, not taking any girl out to dance, but when
he did almost always that girl went with him. If the girl turned
him down, unlike the other men, he never went in pursuit of
another but quietly retraced his steps to the back of the hall, and
soon afterwards he would leave alone. In those years, 'Who will
Eddie Mac try tonight?' was one of the excitements of the
dancehall. He seldom went with the same girl twice.

There was a later time, after it was clear that Annie May was
likely to be running the big Georgian house for a very long time,
when he would ask her to dance because it was politic. 'As an
oul neighbour with another oul neighbour,' he would joke; but
she was cooking him his midday meal now, which he took with
the Kirkwoods in the kitchen. He knew that he could have her
whenever he wanted, but her ample, wholesome looks were too
plain and they lived and worked too close.

Then came another time when the nights Eddie Mac could
dance with the one girl and expect her to go with him
disappeared. Nights came that saw him take girl after girl out,
and none of them would have him. It was not so much that his
dark good looks had coarsened but that he had become too well
known over the years in this small place. And a night eventually
found him dancing with Annie May, no longer 'as an oul
neighbour with another oul neighbour' but as man and woman.
The air was thick with dust that had been carried in on shoes
and beaten into a fine powder; the yellow light gentle from the
tin reflectors behind the row of paraffin lamps around the walls.
The coins had been already counted into a neat stack of blue
paper bags on the card table at the door.

'I suppose I can hardly ask to leave you home since we are
going to the same old place anyhow,' he proposed almost

ruefully, and she found herself blushing all over. It was what she had never dared to hope for all the years.

They passed together through the village, the music from the dancehall still following them; but then the national anthem beat stridently in the night air, and suddenly all was silent. Here and there cautious whispers of lovers drifted from the shelter of walls. The village was mostly sleeping. One thin line of yellow along the blind told that there was after-hour drinking in Charlie's. A man keeping a lookout for the law cast an exploratory cough in their direction at Shivnan's forge, but they went by in silence. As they crossed the stone bridge from the dancehall, they saw the lights of bicycles slowly scattering. Below them, the quiet river slid out in silence towards the level sedgelands and the wilder Shannon.

'Now that they've stood up like fools for the Soldier's Song they can all go home in peace,' Eddie Mac remarked.

After a mile, they left the road and took the path through the fields to the house. It was a dark, windless night, without moon or star, but they could both walk this path in their sleep.

'One good thing about the night is that we're not likely to trip over Master William and his telescope,' Eddie Mac said derisively.

'He's a very educated man,' Annie ventured.

'He's a fool. They're both fools.'

'Maybe it is that they are too educated for land,' she continued uneasily, but he ignored what she had said. Even though they were in the fields, he walked apart from her still, not admitting the bitter blow to his vanity that had been forced to come down to a woman as plain as Annie May after all those years.

'It was different once,' he said suddenly. 'That was long before your time. I was only a boy when Mrs Kirkwood first came to the house. She had been a Miss Darby, old Colonel Darby's daughter. It was an arranged match. The Kirkwoods were almost bankrupt at that time, too – they were never any good – and she had money. The house was done up before she came. It was one of the conditions of the match. The railings were painted, new curtains, everything made shining.

'As soon as they were married, the parties began – bridge parties, tea parties on the lawn. There was a big party every year when the strawberries were ripe. Every Sunday night there was either a dinner party in the house or they went out to some other house to dinner. I heard my father say that old William hated nothing more than those dinners and parties. "It'd make one want to go and live in a cave or under some stone," he said to my father.' Eddie Mac started to laugh. 'All he ever wanted to be with was the bees. The Protestants have always been mad about bees, and there were bee societies at the time. He used to give lectures on bees to the societies. They say the lectures were Mrs Kirkwood's idea. She used always to go with him to the meetings. It was a way of getting him out of the house. Old William never liked to be with people, but Mrs Kirkwood believed in people. "The only reason she goes to church is to meet people," he told my father.'

'Anyhow, he still has his bees,' Annie May said gently.

'Always had, always will have, and now the son has gone the same way, except it's the stars in his case. The only thing you could be certain of is that no matter what he turned to it was bound to be something perfectly useless.'

'The parties had stopped by the time I came,' Annie May said. 'Mrs Kirkwood used to go to the Royal Hotel every Thursday to meet her friends.'

'There weren't enough Protestants left by that time for parties. Once the church in Ardcarne had to be closed it was the beginning of the end. The money Mrs Kirkwood brought was running out too. If I owned their fields, I'd be rolling in money in a few years, and they can't even make ends meet. The whole thing would make a cat laugh.'

'They've been very kind to me,' Annie May said.

'What good did it do them? What good?' he said angrily. 'They're there with one arm as long as the other. Useless to themselves or anybody else. They'll be on the road before long, mark my words, and we'll be with them if we are not careful.'

They had come to the big iron gates of the yard. The gates were chained, and they crossed by the stone stile. The back of the huge house stood away to the left at the head of the yard, and in the darkness, all around them in the yard, were the old stone outhouses. The herdsman's house was some distance beyond the hayshed at the far end of the yard, towards the fields. They stood for a split moment apart on the yard's uneven surface. His natural cunning and vanity still held him back: it was too dangerous, she lived too close to his own doorstep, it could change his life – but his need was too strong.

After that night, around nine every evening, when she had finished the chores, and old William was in bed and Master William reading in the library in the front of the house or out in the fields with his telescope, she would go to the herdsman's house. Too timid to knock, she would make a small scraping sound on the loose door, and sometimes she would have to call. They stayed within the house those first weeks, but after a while he seemed not to want her there. On fine nights, he would take her into the fields. 'We have our own telescope!' And when it rained he still preferred to have her out of the house, though she would have loved to sit with him in the darkness listening to the rain beat on the iron. He would take her across to the dry-stone barn where the fruit was stored, the air sickly sweet with the odour of fermenting apples.

'We can listen to the rain far better here. There's less of roof.'

He kept an old, heavy blanket there above the apple shelves, and he could end the evening whenever he wished. He could not get her out of his own house as easily. The old laws of hospitality were too strong even for him. When he wanted to be rid of her from this neutral storehouse, he could walk her to the corner of the yard across from the big house. Sometimes it seemed to her that the evenings were ending now almost before they began, but she was too ill with desire and fear to complain. A hot Sunday in the middle of June she made her one faint plea for openness or decency.

'Wouldn't it be a good day to take the boat and go on the river?' She was amazed by her own effrontery as soon as the words were spoken. The Kirkwoods had a boathouse on the river and a solid rowboat that was kept in repair but seldom used. To go together on the river would be to bring what had been furtive and hidden into some small light. It would show that he was not ashamed of her. All courting couples went on Sundays to the river in this kind of weather. Even those who couldn't get boats strolled the river bank towards the Oakport Woods. Some of her early admirers had been proud to take her. There were soft bluebells there under the trees, a hidden spring with water so pure it made the teeth chatter even in this heat, and she had drunk it laughing through a stem.

'No. Not today,' he answered slowly, looking down. A yellow

dandelion was growing between the yard stones. He kept moving it forwards and back with his boot.

'Wouldn't it make a change?'

'Not today,' he was still searching for the cover of an acceptable lie. 'There's an animal sick. I wouldn't like to be caught that far from the house if it took a turn for the worse. Anyhow, aren't we as well off round the house here? Maybe later we can ramble down by the orchard. It'll be as cool there as on any river.'

At midday she made a meal that was much liked in this weather – smoked haddock in a cream sauce with cauliflower and young peas and small early potatoes. It must have been all of fourteen years since Mrs Kirkwood had taught her how to bring the sauce to a light consistency, to flavour it with chives and parsley. If Mrs Kirkwood was here on this hot Sunday, William and her son would not be dining with Eddie Mac in the kitchen. The linen and silver would be set in the front room, the front door open, the faded canvas deckchairs stretched under the walnut tree on the front lawn for coffee and newspapers.

The big kitchen, though, was pleasant enough – a fresh coolness from the brown flagstones she had washed in the morning, the door open on the steps down to the yard, a shimmer of heat above the iron roofs, and the dark green of the trees beyond. The house was too big for all of them. The men did not speak as they ate, and she winced as she listened to the thin clink of knife and fork on the bone china.

'I have to say that was a superb meal, Annie,' William volunteered as they rose.

'I can heartily second that,' his son added.

'I'll be around the yard today,' Eddie Mac said to Master William as he lifted his cap. 'I don't like the look of the blue heifer.'

'If you need help, you'll find me in the library.'

She had not eaten, but even after she had cleared the table and washed and put away the dishes she still had little appetite. She drank a mug of coffee with a slice of fruit cake as she stared out on the empty yard. It was already late in the afternoon when she rose, washed the mug, closed the door, and went heavily down the steps into the dull heat of the yard.

She found him at the corner of the stables waiting with an eagerness he hadn't shown for weeks, a blue cloth coat he sometimes wore to the fair on his arm. They went silently into the orchard, picking a place in the high grass away from the beaten path that ran from the gate to the pale row of beehives facing south under the far ivy-covered wall. A clump of wild raspberries that had spread right up to the outer branches of the russet trees gave added cover, though no one in the world would find them there this blessed day.

'You see, it's washed,' he offered her the blue coat to feel with about as much tenderness as it was ever possible for him to show before he spread it on the ground.

'It's as cool here as on any river,' he said as he reached for her. 'As cool as on any river. They can have the fields and anything they want. This is happiness,' he said in a heavy, hoarsely rhythmic tone as he moved above her. 'This is the centre, centre of everything, they can have all else they want.'

'Then I must be part of that centre too,' she said quietly out of the same dull defeat she had felt alone in the big kitchen, not caring about the words she had said.

He stopped in pure amazement. He could not have looked more taken aback if the deep earth itself had stirred and spoken. For a moment, she thought he was about to strike her, but all he did was quickly straighten his clothes and turn his back to her in the long grass. The oppressive silence was at length broken by the sound of the small orchard gate being opened and closed. Old William came slowly down the worn path between the trees. He was going to the hives, dressed all in white, his white beard tucked beneath the suit, the frame of the veil resting on an old straw hat, the long gloves tied with twine below the elbow. He carried a hive tool and smoker, pausing now and then to fan the smoker as he walked slowly along.

From the shelter of the grass and wild canes they watched him go through the hives. His slow care somehow took away some of the oppression. Each time he lifted a roof, a thin stream of bees would move towards the veil. He paid them no attention, working methodically through the hives, sometimes having to use the tool to prize the frames apart, now and again turning his back to the sun to hold up the frames to the light. When he had gone through all the hives, and the bees were quietly working again, he lifted an old wooden chair out of the grass and sat to one side, staring directly into the flight path, the way people lean on bridges to watch water flow below.

'What's he doing?' she asked.

'Nothing. Just watching. He could sit that way for hours. Once I asked him what they were doing. "They're killing off the drones today, Edward," he said. You'd think he was talking about the weather.'

'Still, he sells part of the honey to Sloans,' she said. 'They buy some of his sections every year.'

'For what? For pennies. Mostly he has to feed it back to the bloody bees. Or give it away. The only certain thing about anything the Kirkwoods ever turn their hand to is that it is guaranteed to be perfectly useless.'

They watched old William rise from the chair, remove the hat and veil, freeing a few bees caught in the mesh with his fine, long fingers. He turned the chair upside down again in the grass and came slowly up the orchard. The sun had already gone down behind the walls. They too soon rose, smoothed the stains and bits of grasses from their clothes, and left in opposite directions. Annie May had changed much from the night she had come with Eddie Mac from the dance, but she still held on to a dull hope, and she was beginning to fear that she was with child.

Soon she was certain, and yet she put off telling Eddie. They hired four casual yardmen for the harvest. All her time seemed to go in preparing meals. There was a time when Eddie used to flirt with her in front of the workmen, but now he just ate morosely and silently.

One day she was coming through the yard with a hurriedly gathered bag of green cooking apples for the men's dessert when she heard cheering from the cattle pen. Eddie Mac was in the centre of the pen, his arm round the neck of a young black bull, his free hand gripping its nostrils, the delicate membrane between finger and thumb. The cheering of the men around the pen rose as he slowly forced the struggling animal to its knees, but then suddenly, either through loss of his footing or the terrified animal gathering all its strength into a last surge, he was thrown violently against the steel bars, and the bull broke

loose. He wasn't hurt. He rose at once to race after the bull, to
rain kicks at its mouth and throat, the cornered animal
bellowing for the rest of the herd as it tried to lift its head away
from the blows.

She grew so afraid that she found herself shaking. The fear
stayed with her all through the day as she cooked and served
and washed, and it was to try to lose the fear that she told him in
the evening what she had been putting off for weeks.

He did not look at her as she spoke. He had known from that
first night he took her that it would end with his being driven
out. He had been expecting it from the very beginning. His only
surprise was that it had taken so long.

'How much time is there?' he asked.

'Four months. Maybe a little more.' It was such relief to her
that he had listened so quietly. Then she found herself pressing
for a wild, common happiness. 'We could do up the small
house. Families were brought up in it before. It'd need very little
change. I could go on working in the big house. They'd
probably be only glad of it. It'd mean the two of us were settled.'

'Don't worry. Everything will work itself out,' he said, and
she began to cry. 'We'll have to think things out. It'll take time,'
he said.

'Time?'

'We have to see the priest if we're to be settled. Banns will
have to be read, certificates got, a lot of things. The harvest
business will be all over here in a few days. The yardmen will be
let go at the end of the week. Then we can start to think.'

'Everything will be all right, then,' she could hardly believe
her own happiness.

'You don't have to worry about a single thing. Once this week
is over everything will be taken care of.'

'I was afraid,' she said. 'Now I can't believe that everything is
going to turn out so good.'

He had been through this before. There was only one
difference between this time and the other times. All the other
times it was the girls that had to stir themselves and make for
England. This time he would have to disappear into England.

That night, after she had gone, he lay for a long time fully
clothed on the iron bed in the bare three-roomed house,
smoking cigarette after cigarette, though he usually smoked but

little, staring up at the tongued boards of the ceiling. As a boy he had tried to count right across the ceiling, often by the leaping firelight on a winter's night, but he had never managed to complete a single count, always losing the count among the maze of boards at the centre. Tonight he had no need to count so far. Today had been Monday, the second of the month. Tomorrow: Tuesday. Then Wednesday. The fair of Boyle was held on the first Thursday of every month. That was three days away.

The evening before the fair he picked six of the finest black two-year-olds from the fields, the prize cattle of the farm, and penned them by the road, a rough pen he and his father had put together years before with old railway sleepers. After he closed the pen, he threw hay in a corner so that the cattle would stay quiet through the night. He had been given such a free hand running the land for so long that no one questioned him about the cattle. When he came in it was already dark, and rain had started to fall. He found Annie May ahead of him in the house. Though no lamp was lit, she had stirred the fire and a kettle was boiling. The little table that hung on iron trestles from the wall had been lifted down. Cups and plates were set. She had brought food from the big house.

'As there was no answer, I let myself in,' she apologized.

'You were as well,' he responded.

When she said to him that night, 'You might get finer women, but you'll never find another who'll love you as much as I'll love you,' he knew it to be true in some far-off sense of goodness; but it was not his truth. He saw the child at her breast, the faltering years ahead with the Kirkwoods. He shut it out of his mind.

It was still dark and raining heavily when he put the cattle on the road in the morning. All he had with him was a stick and small bundle. The first miles were the worst. Several times he had to cross into the fields and run alongside the cattle where the walls were broken, their hooves sliding on the road as they raced and checked. It was much easier once they tired and it started to get light. The tanglers looking to buy the cattle cheap before they reached the fair tried to halt him on the outskirts of the town, but with a curse he brushed past them towards the Green. People had put tables and ladders out all along the street to the Green to protect doors and windows. He found a corner along the wall at the very top of the Green. All he had to do now was wait, his clothes stuck to his back with perspiration and rain. As the cattle quietened after their long, hard run, their hooves sore and bleeding, they started to reach up and pluck at the ivy on the wall.

He had to hang around till noon to get the cattle's true price. Though the attempts at bargaining attracted onlookers and attention, to sell the cattle quickly and cheaply would have been even more dangerous still, and it was not his way.

'Do you have any more where those came from?' the big Northern dealer in red cattle boots asked finally as he counted out the notes in a bar off the Green.

'No. Those don't come often,' Eddie Mac replied as he peeled a single note from the wad and handed the luck penny back. The whiskey that sealed the bargain he knocked quickly back. The train was due at three.

Afterwards no one remembered seeing him at the station. He had waited outside among the cars until the train pulled in, and then walked straight on. Each time the tickets were being checked he went to the WC, but he would have paid quietly if challenged. He had more money in his inside pocket than he had ever had in his whole life before.

From Westland Row he walked to the BI terminal on the river and bought a single ticket to Liverpool a few minutes before the boat was due to sail. When the boat was about an hour out to sea, he began to feel cold with the day's tiredness and went to the bar and ordered whiskey. Warmed by the whiskey, he could see as simply back as forward.

The whole place would be ablaze with talk once it got out about the cattle. The Kirkwoods alone would remain quiet. 'His poor father worked here. He was a boy here, grew up here, how could he go and do what he has done,' old William would say. He had nothing against the Kirkwoods, but they were fools. The old lady was the only one with a bit of iron. When Annie May had to tell them the business, they'd no more think of putting her out on the road than they'd be able to put a dog or a cat out. He could even see them start to get fond of the child by the time it started to wander round the big stone house, old William taking it down by the hand to look at the bees.

'Nursing the hard stuff?' a man next to him at the bar enquired.

'That's right.' He didn't want to be drawn into any talk.
'Nursing it well.'

The boat would get into Liverpool in the morning. Though it
would take them days yet to figure out what had happened, he
would travel on to Manchester before getting a haircut and
change of clothes. From Manchester the teeming cities of the
North stretched out: Leeds, Newcastle upon Tyne, Glasgow.
He would get work. He had no need to work for a long time, but
he would still get work. Those not in need always got work
before the people who needed it most. It was a fool's world.

The Sergeant and Guard Deasy would call to the big stone
house. They would write down dates and information in a
notebook and they would search through the herdsman's
house. They would find nothing. A notice would be circulated
for him, with a photo. All the photos they would find would be
old, taken in his footballing days. They would never find him.
Who was ever found out of England! That circular they would
put out would be about as useful as hope in hell.

Manchester, Leeds, Newcastle upon Tyne, Glasgow – they
were like cards spread out on a green table. His only regret was
that he hadn't hit out for one of them years before. He would
miss nothing. If he missed anything, it would probably be the
tongued boards of the ceiling he had never managed to count.
In those cities a man could stay lost forever and victory could
still be found.

Crossing the Line

A few of the last leaves from the almond saplings that stood at intervals along the pavement were being scattered about under the lamps as he met me off the late bus from the city. He was a big man, prematurely bald, and I could feel his powerful tread by my side as we crossed the street to a Victorian cottage, an old vine above its doorway as whimsical there in the very middle of the town as a patch of thyme or lavender.

'The house is tied to the school,' he explained. 'That's why it's not been bulldozed. We don't have any rent to pay.'

His wife looked younger than he, the faded blonde hair and bird face contrasting with her full body. There was about her something of materials faded in the sun. They had two pubescent daughters in convent skirts and blouse, and a son, a few years older than the girls, with the mother's bird-like face and blonde hair, a frail presence beside his father.

'Oliver here will be going back to the uni in a few days. He's doing chemical engineering. He got first-class honours last year, first in his class,' he explained matter-of-factly, to the mother's obvious pleasure and the discomfiture of the son. 'The fees are stiff. They leave things fairly tight just now, but once he's qualified he'll make more in a few years than you and I will ever make in a whole bloody lifetime of teaching. These two great lumps are boarders in The Bower in Athlone. They have a weekend off.' He spoke about his daughters as if he looked upon them already as some other man's future gardens.

'We'd give you tea but the Archdeacon is expecting you. He wants you to have supper with him. I hope you like porridge. Whether you do or not, you better bolt it back like a man and say it was great. As long as you take to the stirabout he'll see nothing much wrong with you. But were you to refuse it, all sorts of moral doubts might start to grow in his old head. He's ninety-eight, the second oldest priest in the whole of Ireland, but he'll tell you all this himself. I'd better leave you there now before he starts to worry. The one thing you have to remember is to address yourself like a boy to the stirabout.'

The wind had died a little outside. We walked up the wide street, thronged with people in from the country for the late Saturday shopping. There were queues outside the butcher's, the baker's, within the chemist's. Music came from some of the bars. Everywhere there was much greeting and stopping. Pale-faced children seemed to glide about between the shops in the shadow of their mothers. Some of these raised diffident hands or called, 'Master Kennedy', to the big man by my side, and he seemed to know them all by name.

One rather well-dressed old man alone passed us in open hostility. It was so much in marked contrast to the general friendliness that I asked, 'What's wrong with *him*?'

'He's a teacher from out the country. They don't like me. I'm not in their bloody union. Are you in the INTO by any chance?'

'They offered us a special rate before leaving college. Everybody joined.'

'That's your own business, of course. I never found it much use,' he said irritably.

He left me outside the heavy iron gates of the presbytery. 'Call in on your way back to tell us how you got on. Then I'll bring you down to your digs.'

A light above the varnished door shone on white gravel and the thick hedge of laurel and rhododendron that appeared to hide a garden or lawn. A housekeeper led me into the front room where a very old white-haired priest sat over a coal fire.

'You're from the west – a fine dramatic part of the country, but no fit place at all to live, no depth of soil. Have you ever heard of William Bulfin?' he asked as soon as I was seated by his side.

'*Rambles in Eirinn?*' I remembered.

'For my ordination I was given a present of a Pierce bicycle. I rode all around Ireland that summer on the new Pierce with a copy of the *Rambles*. It was a very weary-dreary business pedalling through the midlands, in spite of the rich land. I could feel my heart lift, though, when at last I got to the west. It's still no place to live. Have you met Mr Kennedy?'

'Yes, Father. He showed me here.'

'Does he find you all right?'

'I think so, Father.'

'That's good enough for me, then. Do you think you'll be happy here?'

'I think so, Father.'

'I expect you'll see out my time. I thought the last fellow would, but he left. I dislike changes. I'm ninety-eight years old. There's only one priest older in the whole of Ireland, a Father Michael Kelly from the Diocese of Achonry. He's a hundred-and-two. You might have noticed the fuss when he reached the hundred?'

'I must have missed it, Father.'

'I would have imagined that to be difficult. I thought it excessive, but I take a special interest in him. Kelly is the first name I look for every morning on the front of the *Independent*,' he smiled slyly.

The housekeeper came into the room with a steaming saucepan, two bowls, a jug of milk and water, which she set on a low table between our chairs. Then she took a pair of glasses and a bottle of Powers from a press, and withdrew.

'I don't drink, Father,' I said as he raised the bottle.

'You're wise. The heart doesn't need drink at your age. I didn't touch it till I was forty, but after forty I think every man should drink a little. The heart needs a jab or two every day to remind it of its business once it crosses forty. What do you think the business of the heart is?'

'I suppose it has many businesses, Father.'

'You'll never be convicted on that answer, son, but it has only one main business. That's to keep going. If it doesn't do that all its other businesses can be forgotten about.'

He poured himself a very large whiskey, which he drank neat, and then added a smaller measure, filling the glass with water. The Principal had been right. The saucepan was full of steaming porridge when he lifted the lid. He ladled it into the bowls with a wooden spoon, leaving place enough in the bowl for milk and a sprinkling of sugar. It was all I could do to finish what was in the bowl. I noticed how remarkably steady his hand was as he brought the spoon to his lips.

'If a man sticks to the stirabout he's unlikely to go very far wrong,' he concluded. 'I hope you'll be happy here. Mr

Kennedy is a good man. He went on our side in that strike. He kept the school open. It was presumably good for the pupils. I think, though, it brought some trouble on himself. It's seldom wise in the long run to go against your own crowd.'

He'd risen, laying his rug aside, but before I could leave he took me by the shoulder up to a large oil painting in a heavy gilt frame above the mantel. 'Look at it carefully. What do you see?'

'A tropical tree. It looks like an island.'

'Look again. It's a trick painting,' he said, and when I could make nothing more of it he traced lines from the tree, which also depicted a melancholy military figure in a cocked hat. 'Napoleon, on Elba,' he laughed.

The Kennedys had invited me to their Sunday lunch the next day. Their kitchen was pleasant and extremely warm, the two girls setting the big table, and smells of roasting chicken and apple stew coming from the black-leaded range. There was wine with the meal, a sweet white wine. Afterwards, the girls cleared the table and, asking permission, disappeared into the town. Oliver sat on in the room. Kennedy filled his wife's glass to the brim with the last of the Sauterne, rose, and got himself a whiskey from the press in place of the wine.

'You were just like he was twenty-one years ago. Your first school. Straight from the training college. Starting out,' Mrs Kennedy said, her face pink with the wine and cooking.

'Teachers' jobs were hard come by in those days. Temporary assistant teacher for one year in the Marist Brothers in Sligo was my first job. There was pay but you could hardly call it pay. Not enough to keep a wren alive.'

'It was the first of July. I remember it well. We had a bar and grocery by the harbour and sold newspapers. He came in for the *Independent*. He was tall then, with a thick head of brown hair. I know it was the first of July, but I forget the year.'

'Nineteen thirty-three. It was the year I got out of college. I bought that *Independent* to see if there were any permanent jobs coming up in October.'

'We were both only twenty. They told us to wait till we had saved some money, that we had plenty of time. But we couldn't wait. My father gave us two rooms above the grocery part of the shop. Do you ever regret not waiting?'

'We wouldn't have saved anyhow. There was nothing to save. And we had those years.'

I felt an intruder. Their son sat there, shamed and fascinated, unable to cry stop, or tear himself away.

'Those two rooms were rotten with damp, and when there were storms you should have heard the damned panes. You could have wallpapered the rooms with the number of letters beginning "The Manager regrets" that came through the letterbox that winter. Oliver here was on the way.'

'Those two rooms were happiness,' she said, lifting the glass of sweet wine to her lips, while her son writhed with unease on the sofa.

'We could get no job, and then I was suddenly offered three at the same time. It's always the same. You either get more than you want or you get nothing. We came here because the house went with the school. It meant a great deal in those days. It still does us no harm.'

I walked with Kennedy to the school on the Monday. He introduced me to the classes I was to teach. We walked together on the concrete during the mid-morning break. Eagerly, he started to talk as we walked up and down among the playing children. The regulation ten minutes ran to twenty before he rang the bell.

'They're as well playing in this weather. The inspectors never try to catch me out. They know the work gets done.'

It was the same at the longer lunchtime, the talk veering again to the early days of his marriage.

'I used to go back to those two rooms for lunch. We'd just go straight to bed, grabbing a sandwich on the way out. Sometimes we had it off against the edge of the table. It was a great feeling afterwards, walking about with the Brothers, knowing that they'd never have it in the whole of their lives.'

I walked with him on that concrete in total silence. I must have been close to the perfect listener for this excited, forceful man. No one had ever spoken to me like this before. I didn't know what to say. The children milled about us in the weak sun. Sometimes I shivered at the premonition that days like this might be a great part of the rest of my life, and I had dreamed once that through teaching I would help make the world a better place.

'What made you take up teaching?' he asked. 'I know the hours are good enough, and there's the long holidays, but what the hell good is it without money?'

'I don't know why,' I answered. 'Some notion of service . . . of doing good.'

'It's easy to see that you're young. Teaching is a lousy, tiring old job, and it gets worse as you get older. A new bunch comes at you year after year. They stay the same but you start to go down. You'll not get thanked for service in this world. There were no jobs when I was young. It was considered a bloody miracle to have any sort of a job with a salary. If I was in your boots now I'd do something like dentistry or engineering, even if I had to scrape for the money.'

The time had already gone several minutes past the lunchtime. The children were whirling about us on the concrete in loud abandon, for them the minutes of play stolen from the schoolday were pure sweetness.

'Still, if I had had those chances, I wouldn't have gone to Sligo and I'd never have met her,' he mused.

I was in my room in the digs after tea one evening when a daughter of the house in the blouse and gymfrock of the convent secondary school knocked and said, 'There's a visitor for you in the front room downstairs.'

A frail, grey-haired man rose as soon as I entered. He had an engaging handshake and smile.

'I'm Owen Beirne, branch secretary of the INTO. I just called in to welcome you to the town and to invite you to our meeting on Friday night. I teach in a small school out in the country. Forgive the speech.' He smiled as he sat down.

I explained briefly that I had joined the union already and suggested that we move from the stiff front room.

'We'll cross in a minute to the Bridge Bar. They always have a nice fire, but it's safer to say what I have to say here. I suppose you don't know about your Principal and the union.'

'He told me he wasn't a member.'

'Did he try to stop you joining?' he asked sharply.

'No. I told him I'd joined already.'

'Well, he was a member before the strike, but he refused to come out on strike. For several months he crossed that picket line, while the church and de Valera tried to starve us to our knees.'

There was nothing for me to say.

'As far as we are concerned, I mean the rest of the teachers around here, Kennedy doesn't exist. You're in a different position. He's your Principal. You have to work with the man. But if we were to meet the two of you together, you might find yourself blackballed as well.'

'I don't mind.'

'It means nothing as far as you are concerned. You just go your own way and notice nothing. But should he try to pull the heavy on you in school – he did with one of your predecessors – let us know and we'll fall on him like the proverbial load of bricks.' He had risen. 'That's what I wanted to get out of the way.'

The bar was empty, but there was a bright fire of logs at one end. Owen Beirne ordered a hot whiskey with cloves and lemon. The barman seemed to like and respect him. I had a glass of lemonade.

'Don't you take a drink?'

'Seldom.'

'I drink too much. It's expensive and a waste of time. During the times I don't drink, I read far more and feel better in every way. Unfortunately, it's very pleasant.'

He told me his father had been a teacher. 'My poor father had to go to the back door of the presbytery every month for his pay. The priest's housekeeper gave it to him. It was four pounds in those days. I'll never forget my mother's face when he came back from the presbytery one night with three pounds instead of four. The housekeeper had held back a pound because the priest had decided to paint the church that month. One of the great early things the INTO got for the teacher was for the salary to be paid directly into his own hands – to get it through the post instead of from the priest or his housekeeper.

'All that was changed by my time. The inspectors, the dear inspectors, were our hairshirts. A recurring nightmare I have is walking up and down in front of a class with an inspector sitting at the back quietly taking notes. Some were the roaring boys. One rode the bucking mule in Duffy's Circus in Ballinasloe, got badly thrown, but was still out before nine the next morning to check if the particular teacher he'd been drinking with was on

time. They were like lords or judges. Full-grown men trembled
in front of them at these annual inspections. Women were often
in tears. The best hams and fruit cakes were brought out at
lunchtime. For some there had to be the whiskey bottle and
stout in the schoolhouse after school.

'Then, during the war, the Emergency, we had an inspector in
Limerick called Deasy, a fairly young man. I was teaching in his
area at the time. He was a real rat. In Newcastle West there was
an old landed family, a racehorse and gambling crowd, down on
their luck. An uncle was the Bishop of Cashel. One of the sons
was a failed medical student, and God knows what else, and as
part of a rehabilitation scheme didn't the Bishop get him a
temporary teaching job. Deasy was his inspector. I'm sure the
teaching was choice, and what Deasy didn't say to his man
wasn't worth saying. This crowd wasn't used to being talked to
like that. He just walked out of the school without saying a
word. Deasy sat down to his tea and ham sandwiches and fruit
cake with the schoolmistress. They were still having lunch when
your man arrived back. He sat down with them, opened his coat
nice and quietly, produced the shotgun and gave Deasy both
barrels. He wasn't even offered the Act of Contrition. I was in
the cathedral in Limerick the night Deasy's body was brought
in. It was a sad sight, the widow and seven children behind the
coffin. Every inspector in the country was at the funeral. Things
were noticeably easier afterwards.'

'What happened to your man?'

'He was up for murder. He'd have swung at the time but for the
Bishop, who got him certified. They say that after a few years he
was spirited away to Australia. He was as sane as I was.'

'It seems to be a more decent time now,' I said.

'It's by no means great, but it's certainly better than it was.'

A few people had come into the bar by this time. They looked
our way but no one joined us at the fire. He'd had four drinks,
and his face was flushed and excited. He wanted to know what
poets my generation was reading. He seemed unimpressed by
the names I mentioned. His own favourite was Horace.
'Sometimes I translate him for fun, as a kind of discipline. I
always feel in good spirits afterwards.'

Almost absently he spilled out a number of coloured capsules
from a small plastic container on to the table, got a glass of water

from the bar. 'It's the old ticker. I'm afraid it's wobbly. But I hope not to embarrass my friends,' he said.

'I'm sorry. That's lousy luck to have.'

'There's no need,' he answered laughing as we took leave of one another. 'I've had good innings.'

Kennedy didn't call to the digs next morning, and I made my own way to the school. As I came through the gates I saw that he had all the classes lined up on the concrete, and he was looking so demonstratively at his watch that I checked the time on my own watch. I was in time but only just. Before I got any closer he'd marched his own classes in, disappearing behind a closed door. Instead of coming round with the roll books that morning, he sent one of the senior boys, and at the mid-morning break I found myself alone on the concrete for several minutes, but when he did join me his grievance spilled out at once.

'I heard yourself and Mr Beirne had a long session in the Bridge House last night.'

'He called at the digs. It was more comfortable to cross to the Bridge.'

'I suppose plenty of dirt was fired in my direction.'

'None. He said the fact that you're not in the INTO must be no concern of mine. It was the only time you were mentioned.'

'That was very good of him. There are many people around here who would think him not fit company for a young teacher,' he said angrily.

'Why?'

'Every penny he has goes on booze or books and some of the books are far from edifying, by all accounts. He's either out every night in the bars, or else he shuts himself off for weeks on end. They say his wife was dead in the house for most of a day before he noticed. The priests certainly think he's no addition to the place.'

'He seemed an intelligent man.'

'He knows how to put on a good front, all right.'

'He seemed very decent to me,' I refused to give way.

'He's no friend of mine. You can take my word for that. All that crowd would have my guts for garters if they got the chance. They'll have a long wait, I can tell you. When I came to this town we hadn't two coins to slink together. Every morsel of food we put in our mouths that first month here was on credit. But I worked. Every hour of private tuition going round the place I took, and that's the lousiest of all teaching jobs, face to face for a whole hour with a well-heeled dunce. Then I got surveying work with the solicitors. I must have walked half the fields within miles of this town with the chains. I was just about on my feet when that strike was called. The children were in good schools. Why should I put all that at risk? It wasn't my strike. Some of the ones that went on strike will be in hock for the rest of their days. And if it had lasted even another month they'd have had to crawl back like beaten dogs. Do you think it was easy for me to pass those pickets with their placards and cornerboy jeers every schoolday for the whole of seven months? Do you think that was easy?'

'I know it wasn't easy.'

There was a Mass that Friday for the teachers and children of the parish, an official blessing on the new year, and we were given the day off to attend the Mass. Kennedy called for me and we walked up the town together to the church. At the top of Main Street, we ran straight into Owen Beirne. Rather than cut us openly, he crossed to a fish stall and pretended to be examining the freshness of a tray of plaice as we went by.

'Your friend Beirne hadn't much to say to you today. You were in the wrong company.'

'I don't mind,' I said.

As we came up to the railings of the church, a red-faced hulk of a man, obviously a teacher, the gold *fáinne* and metal tricolour in his lapel, stared at Kennedy in open hostility, cleared his throat, and spat out into our path. Kennedy said nothing as we hurried into the church. After Mass little groups of teachers stood about in the church grounds, shaking hands, joking, but as soon as we approached they fell silent or turned away. Not a single person spoke to us or raised a hat or even bowed. We passed out in total silence. I had never run such a gauntlet. I had the feeling as we walked back through the town that Kennedy was desperately searching for something to say but that he was too disturbed to settle on any one phrase.

'You might as well come into my place for a cup of tea or something,' he said eventually. 'You have a good hour yet to go till your lunch.'

His house was empty and he made the tea himself. 'They can try as hard as they are able but they can't harm me now,' he began slowly as he made the tea. 'In another two years Oliver will be qualified. By that time, the pair of girls will be on their way into the Civil Service or training college. That summer we'll buy the car. We could buy it even now but we decided to wait till we could do it right. It'll be no secondhand. That summer we'll take the first holiday since we were married. We'll drive all round Ireland, staying in the best hotels. We'll not spare or stint on anything. We'll have wine, prawns or smoked salmon, sole or lobster or sirloin or lamb, anything on the menu we feel like no matter what the price.'

I was beginning to think that people grow less spiritual the older they were, contrary to what is thought. It was as if some desire to plunge their arms up to the elbow into the steaming entrails of the world grew more fierce the closer they got to leaving. It was a very different dream to the young priest's, cycling round Ireland with a copy of the 'Rambles' all those years ago.

'Have you noticed Eileen O'Reilly?' he changed as we sat with the cups of tea.

'She's very pretty,' I said.

Eileen O'Reilly worked in one of the solicitor's offices. She was small and blonde with a perfect figure. I thought she'd smiled at me as she passed on a bicycle during a lunch hour. She was standing on the pedals to force the bike across the hill.

'If I was in your place, I'd go for her,' he said wistfully. 'She has no steady boyfriend. I do surveying for her office and we always have a joke or an old flirt. When I brought up your name a few days back she blushed beetroot. I can tell she's interested in you. In two years Oliver will be qualified and I'll have no more need of the surveying. I could hand it over to you. You'd not be rich, but with the fees on top of the teaching you'd be very comfortable for a young man. You could well afford to marry. I'd not leave her hanging around long if I was in your boots. In two years' time if you stayed on at the school here and married Eileen I'd give you the surveying. There's nothing to it once you get the knack of the chains.'

High Ground

I let the boat drift on the river beneath the deep arch of the bridge, the keel scraping the gravel as it crossed the shallows out from Walsh's, past the boathouse at the mouth, and out into the lake. It was only the slow growing distance from the ring of reeds round the shore that told that the boat moved at all on the lake. More slowly still, the light was going from the August evening.

I was feeling leaden with tiredness but did not want to sleep. I had gone on the river in order to be alone, the way one goes to a darkroom.

The Brothers' Building Fund Dance had been held the night before. A big marquee had been set up in the grounds behind the monastery. Most of the people I had gone to school with were there, awkward in their new estate, and nearly all the brothers who had taught us: Joseph, Francis, Benedictus, Martin. They stood in a black line beneath the low canvas near the entrance and waited for their old pupils to go up to them. When they were alone, watching us dance, rapid comment passed up and down the line, and often Joseph and Martin doubled up, unable or unwilling to conceal laughter; but by midnight they had gone, and a night of a sort was ours, the fine dust from the floor rising into the perfume and sweat and hair oil as we danced in the thresh of the music.

There was a full moon as I drove Una to her home in Arigna in the borrowed Prefect, the whole wide water of Allen taking in the wonderful mysteriousness of the light. We sat in the car and kissed and talked, and morning was there before we noticed. After the harshness of growing up, a world of love and beauty, of vague gardens and dresses and laughter, one woman in a gleaming distance seemed to be almost within reach. We would enter this world. We would make it true.

I was home just before the house had risen, and lay on the bed and waited till everybody was up, and then changed into old clothes. I was helping my father put a new roof on the house. Because of the tiredness, I had to concentrate completely on the work, even then nearly losing my footing several times between the stripped beams, sometimes annoying my father by handing him the wrong lath or tool; but when evening came the last thing I wanted was sleep. I wanted to be alone, to go over the night, to try to see clearly, which only meant turning again and again in the wheel of dreaming.

'Hi there! Hi! Do you hear me, young Moran!' The voice came with startling clarity over the water, was taken up by the fields across the lake, echoed back. 'Hi there! Hi! Do you hear me, young Moran!'

I looked all around. The voice came from the road. I couldn't make out the figure at first, leaning in a broken gap of the wall above the lake, but when he called again I knew it was Eddie Reegan. Senator Reegan.

'Hi there, young Moran. Since the mountain can't come to Mahomet, Mahomet will have to come to the mountain. Row over here for a minute. I want to have a word with you.'

I rowed very slowly, watching each oar splash slip away from the boat in the mirror of water. I disliked him, having unconsciously, perhaps, picked up my people's dislike. He had come poor to the place, buying Lynch's small farm cheap, and soon afterwards the farmhouse burned down. At once, a bigger house was built with the insurance money, closer to the road, though that in its turn was due to burn down too, to be replaced by the present mansion, the avenue of Lawson cypresses now seven years old. Soon he was buying up other small farms, but no one had ever seen him work with shovel or with spade. He always appeared immaculately dressed. It was as if he understood instinctively that it was only the shortest of short steps from appearance to becoming. 'A man who works never makes any money. He has no time to see how the money is made,' he was fond of boasting. He set up as an auctioneer. He entered politics. He married Kathleen Relihan, the eldest of old Paddy Relihan's daughters, the richest man in the area, Chairman of the County Council. 'Do you see those two girls? I'm going to marry one of those girls,' he was reported to have remarked to a friend. 'Which one?' 'It doesn't matter. They're both Paddy Relihan's daughters'; and when Paddy retired it was Reegan rather than any of his own sons who succeeded Paddy in the Council. Now that he had surpassed Paddy Relihan and become a Senator, and it seemed only a matter of time before he was elected to the Dail, he no longer joked about 'the aul effort of a fire', and was gravely concerned about the reluctance of insurance companies to grant cover for fire to dwelling houses in our part of the country. He had bulldozed the hazel and briar from the hills above the lake, and as I turned to see how close the boat had come to the wall I could see behind him the white and black of his Friesians grazing between the electric fences on the far side of the reseeded hill.

I let the boat turn so that I could place my hand on the stone, but the evening was so calm that it would have rested beneath the high wall without any hand. The Senator had seated himself on the wall as I was rowing in, and his shoes hung six or eight feet above the boat.

'It's not the first time I've had to congratulate you, though I'm too high up here to shake your hand. And what I'm certain of is that it won't be the last time either,' he began.

'Thanks. You're very kind,' I answered.

'Have you any idea where you'll go from here?'

'No. I've applied for the grant. It depends on whether I get the grant or not.'

'What'll you do if you get it?'

'Go on, I suppose. Go a bit farther. . . .'

'What'll you do then?'

'I don't know. Sooner or later, I suppose, I'll have to look for a job.'

'That's the point I've been coming to. You are qualified to teach, aren't you?'

'Yes. But I've only taught for a few months. Before I got that chance to go to the University.'

'You didn't like teaching?' he asked sharply.

'No.' I was careful. 'I didn't dislike it. It was a job.'

'I like that straightness. And what I'm looking to know is – if you were offered a very good job would you be likely to take it?'

'What job?'

'I won't beat around the bush either. I'm talking of the Principalship of the school here. It's a very fine position for a young man. You'd be among your own people. You'd be doing good where you belong. I hear you're interested in a very attractive young lady not a hundred miles from here. If you decided to marry and settle down I'm in a position to put other advantages your way.'

Master Leddy was the Principal of the school. He had been the Principal as long as I could remember. He had taught me, many before me. I had called to see him just three days before. The very idea of replacing him was shocking. And anyhow, I knew the politicians had nothing to do with the appointment of teachers. It was the priest who ran the school. What he was saying didn't even begin to make sense, but I had been warned about his cunning and was wary. 'You must be codding. Isn't Master Leddy the Principal?'

'He is now but he won't be for long more – not if I have anything to do with it.'

'How?' I asked very quietly in the face of the outburst.

'That need be no concern of yours. If you can give me your word that you'll take the job, I can promise you that the job is as good as yours.'

'I can't do that. I can't follow anything right. Isn't it Canon Gallagher who appoints the teachers?'

'Listen. There are many people who feel the same way as I do. If I go to the Canon in the name of all those people and say that you're willing to take the job, the job is yours. Even if he didn't want to, he'd have no choice but to appoint you. . . .'

'Why should you want to do that for me? Say, even if it is possible.' I was more curious now than alarmed.

'It's more than possible. It's bloody necessary. I'll be plain. I have three sons. They go to that school. They have nothing to fall back on but whatever education they get. And with the education they're getting at that school up there, all they'll ever be fit for is to dig ditches. Now, I've never dug ditches, but even at my age I'd take off my coat and go down into a ditch rather than ever have to watch any of my sons dig. The whole school is a shambles. Someone described it lately as one big bear garden.'

'What makes you think I'd be any better?'

'You're young. You're qualified. You're ambitious. It's a very good job for someone of your age. I'd give you all the backing you'd want. You'd have every reason to make a go of it. With you there, I'd feel my children would be still in with a chance. In another year or two even that'll be gone.'

'I don't see why you want my word at this stage,' I said evasively, hoping to slip away from it all. I saw his face return to its natural look of shrewdness in what was left of the late summer light.

'If I go to the Canon now, it'll be just another complaint in a long line of complaints. If I can go to him and say that things can't be allowed to go on as they have been going and we have a young man here, from a good family, a local, more than qualified, who's willing to take the job, who has everyone's backing, it's a different proposition entirely. And I can guarantee you here this very evening that you'll be the Principal of that school when it opens in September.'

For the first time it was all coming clear to me.

'What'll happen to the Master? What'll he do?'

'What I'm more concerned about is what'll my children do if he stays,' he burst out again. 'But you don't have to concern yourself about it. It'll be all taken care of.'

I had called on the Master three evenings before, walking beyond the village to the big ramshackle farmhouse. He was just rising, having taken all his meals of the day in bed, and was shaving and dressing upstairs, one time calling down for a towel, and again for a laundered shirt.

'Is that young Moran?' He must have recognized my voice or name. 'Make him a good cup of tea. And he'll be able to be back up the road with myself.'

A very old mongrel greyhound was routed from the leather armchair one side of the fire, and I was given tea and slices of buttered bread. The Master's wife, who was small and frail with pale skin and lovely brown eyes, kept up a cheerful chatter that required no response as she busied herself about the enormous cluttered kitchen which seemed not to possess a square foot of room. There were buckets everywhere, all sorts of chairs, basins, bags of meal and flour, cats, the greyhound, pots and pans. The pattern had faded from the bulging wallpaper, a dark ochre, and some of the several calendars that hung around the walls had faded into the paper. It would have been difficult to find space for an extra cup or saucer on the long wooden table. There were plainly no set meal times. Two of the Master's sons, now grown men, came singly in from the fields while I waited. Plates of food were served at once, bacon and liver, a mug of tea. They took from the plate of bread already on the table, the butter, the sugar, the salt, the bottle of sauce. They spent no more than a few minutes over the meal, blessing themselves at its end, leaving as suddenly as they'd entered, smiling and nodding in a friendly way in my direction, but making little attempt at conversation, though Gerald did ask, before he reached for his hat – a hat I recognized as having belonged to the Master back in my school days, a brown hat with a blue teal's feather and a small hole burned in its side – 'Well, how are things getting along in the big smoke?' The whole effect was of a garden and orchard gone completely wild, but happily.

'You couldn't have come at a better time. We'll be able to be up the road together,' the Master said as he came heavily down the stairs in his stockinged feet. He'd shaved, was dressed in a grey suit, with a collar and tie, the old gold watch-chain crossing a heavy paunch. He had failed since last I'd seen him, the face red and puffy, the white hair thinned, and there was a bruise on the cheekbone where he must have fallen. The old hound went towards him, licking at his hand.

'Good boy! Good boy,' he said as he came towards me, patting the hound. As soon as we shook hands he slipped his feet into shoes which had stood beside the leather chair. He did not bend or sit, and as he talked I saw the small bird-like woman at his feet, tying up the laces.

'It's a very nice thing to see old pupils coming back. Though not many of them bring me laurels like yourself, it's still a very nice thing. Loyalty is a fine quality. A very fine quality.'

'Now,' his wife stood by his side, 'all you need is your hat and stick,' and she went and brought them.

'Thank you. Thank you indeed. I don't know what I'd do but for my dear wife,' he said.

'Do you hear him now! He was never stuck for the charm. Off with you now before you get the back of me hand,' she bantered, and called as we went slowly towards the gate. 'Do you want me to send any of the boys up for you?'

'No. Not unless they have some business of their own to attend to in the village. No,' he said gravely, turning very slowly.

He spoke the whole way on the slow walk to the village. All the time he seemed to lag behind my snail's pace, sometimes standing because he was out of breath, tapping at the road with the cane. Even when the walk slowed to a virtual standstill it seemed to be still far too energetic.

'I always refer to you as my star pupil. When the whole enterprise seems to be going more or less askew, I always point to young Moran: that's one good job I turned out. Let the fools prate.'

I walked, stooping by his side, restraining myself within the slow walk, embarrassed, ashamed, confused. I had once looked to him in pure infatuation, would rush to his defence against every careless whisper. He had shone like a clear star. I was in love with what I hardly dared to hope I might become. It seemed horrible now that I might come to this.

'None of my own family were clever,' he confided. 'It was a great disappointment. And yet they may well be happier for it. Life is an extraordinary thing. A very great mystery. Wonderful . . . shocking . . . thing.'

Each halting speech seemed to lead in some haphazard way into the next.

'Now that you're coming out into the world you'll have to be constantly on your guard. You'll have to be on your guard first of all against intellectual pride. That's the worst sin, the sin of Satan. And always be kind to women. Help them. Women are weak. They'll be attracted to you.' I had to smile ruefully, never having noticed much of a stampede in my direction. 'There was this girl I left home from a dance once,' he continued. 'And as we were getting closer to her house I noticed her growing steadily more amorous until I had to say, "None of that now, girl. It is not the proper time!" Later, when we were both old and married, she thanked me. She said I was a true gentleman.'

The short walk seemed to take a deep age, but once outside Ryan's door he took quick leave of me. 'I won't invite you inside. Though I set poor enough of an example, I want to bring

no one with me. I say to all my pupils: Beware of the high stool.
The downward slope from the high stool is longer and steeper
than from the top of Everest. God bless and guard you, young
Moran. Come and see me again before you head back to the
city.' And with that he left me. I stood facing the opaque glass of
the door, the small print of the notice above it: *Seven Days Licence
to Sell Wine, Beer, Spirits*.

'Do you mean the Master'll be out on the road, then?' I asked
Senator Reegan from the boat, amazed still by the turn of the
conversation.

'You need have no fear of that. There's a whole union behind
him. In our enlightened day alcoholism is looked upon as just
another illness. And they wonder how the country can be so
badly off,' he laughed sarcastically. 'No. He'll probably be
offered a rest cure on full pay. I doubt if he'd take it. If he did,
it'd delay official recognition of your appointment by a few
months, that'd be all, a matter of paperwork. The very worst
that could happen to him is that he'd be forced to take early
retirement, which would probably add years to his life. He'd
just have that bit less of a pension with which to drink himself
into an early grave. You need have no worries on that score.
You'd be doing everybody a favour, including him most of all, if
you'd take the job. Well, what do you say? I could still go to the
Canon tonight. It's late but not too late. He'd be just addressing
himself to his hot toddy. It could be as good a time as any to
attack him. Well, what do you say?'

'I'll have to think about it.'

'It's a very fine position for a young man like yourself starting
out in life.'

'I know it is. I'm very grateful.'

'To hell with gratitude. Gratitude doesn't matter a damn. It's
one of those moves that benefits everybody involved. You'll
come to learn that there aren't many moves like that in life.'

'I'll have to think about it.' I was anxious to turn away from
any direct confrontation.

'I can't wait for very long. Something has to be done and done
soon.'

'I know that but I still have to think about it.'

'Listen. Let's not close on anything this evening. Naturally you have to consider everything. Why don't you drop over to my place tomorrow night? You'll have a chance to meet my lads. And herself has been saying for a long time now that she'd like to meet you. Come about nine. Everything will be out of the way by then.'

I rowed very slowly away, just stroking the boat forward in the deadly silence of the half-darkness. I watched Reegan cross the road, climb the hill, pausing now and then among the white blobs of his Friesians. His figure stood for a while at the top of the hill where he seemed to be looking back towards the boat and water before he disappeared.

When I got back to the house everyone was asleep except a younger sister, who had waited up for me. She was reading by the fire, the small black cat on her knee.

'They've all gone to bed,' she explained. 'Since you were on the river, they let me wait up for you. Only there's no tea. I've just found out that there's not a drop of spring water in the house.'

'I'll go to the well, then. Otherwise someone will have to go first thing in the morning. You don't have to wait up for me.' I was too agitated to go straight to bed and glad of the distraction of any activity.

'I'll wait,' she said. 'I'll wait and make the tea when you get back.'

'I'll be less than ten minutes.' The late hour held for her the attractiveness of the stolen.

I walked quickly, swinging the bucket. The whole village seemed dead under a benign moon, but as I passed along the church wall I heard voices. They came from Ryan's Bar. It was shut, the blinds down, but then I noticed cracks of yellow light along the edges of the big blue blind. They were drinking after hours. I paused to see if I could recognize any of the voices, but before I had time Charlie Ryan hissed, 'Will you keep your voices down, will yous? At the rate you're going you'll soon have the Sergeant out of his bed,' and the voices quietened to a whisper. Afraid of being noticed in the silence, I passed on to get the bucket of spring water from the well, but the voices were in full song again by the time I returned. I let the bucket softly down in the dust and stood in the shadow of the church wall to listen. I recognized the Master's slurred voice at once, and then voices of some of the men who worked the sawmill in the wood.

'That sixth class in 1933 was a great class, Master.' It was Johnny Connor's voice, the saw mechanic. 'I was never much good at the Irish, but I was a terror at the maths, especially the Euclid.'

I shivered as I listened under the church wall. Nineteen thirty-three was the year before I was born.

'You were a topper, Johnny. You were a topper at the maths,' I heard the Master's voice. It was full of authority. He seemed to have no sense at all that he was in danger.

'Tommy Morahan that went to England was the best of us all in that class,' another voice took up, a voice I wasn't able to recognize.

'He wasn't half as good as he imagined he was. He suffered from a swelled head,' Johnny Connor said.

'Ye were toppers, now. Ye were all toppers,' the Master said diplomatically.

'One thing sure is that you made a great job of us, Master. You were a powerful teacher. I remember to this day everything you told us about the Orinoca River.'

'It was no trouble. Ye had the brains. There are people in this part of the country digging ditches who could have been engineers or doctors or judges or philosophers had they been given the opportunity. But the opportunity was lacking. That was all that was lacking.' The Master spoke again with great authority.

'The same again all round, Charlie,' a voice ordered. 'And a large brandy for the Master.'

'Still, we kept sailing, didn't we, Master? That's the main thing. We kept sailing.'

'Ye had the brains. The people in this part of the country had powerful brains.'

'If you had to pick one thing, Master, what would you put those brains down to?'

'Will you hush now! The Sergeant wouldn't even have to be passing outside to hear yous. Soon he'll be hearing yous down in the barracks,' Charlie hissed.

There was a lull again in the voices in which a coin seemed to roll across the floor.

'Well, the people with the brains mostly stayed here. They had to. They had no choice. They didn't go to the cities. So the brains was passed on to the next generation. Then there's the trees. There's the water. And we're very high up here. We're practically at the source of the Shannon. If I had to pick on one thing more than another, I'd put it down to that. I'd attribute it to the high ground.'

Gold Watch

It was in Grafton Street we met, aimlessly strolling in one of the lazy lovely Saturday mornings in spring, the week of work over, the weekend still as fresh as the bunch of anemones that seemed the only purchase in her cane shopping basket.

'What a lovely surprise,' I said.

I was about to take her hand when a man with an armload of parcels parted us as she was shifting the basket to her other hand, and we withdrew out of the pushing crowds into the comparative quiet of Harry Street. We had not met since we had graduated in the same law class from University College five years before. I had heard she'd become engaged to the medical student she used to knock around with, and had gone into private practice down the country, perhaps, waiting for him to graduate.

'Are you up for the weekend or on holiday or what?' I asked.

'No. I work here now.' She named a big firm that specialized in tax law. 'I felt I needed a change.'

She was wearing a beautiful suit, the colour of oatmeal, the narrow skirt slit from the knee. The long gold hair of her student days was drawn tightly into a neat bun at the back.

'You look different but as beautiful as ever,' I said. 'I thought you'd be married by now.'

'And do you still go home every summer?' she countered, perhaps out of confusion.

'It doesn't seem as if I'll ever break that bad habit.'

We had coffee in Bewley's – the scent of the roasting beans blowing through the vents out on to Grafton Street forever mixed with the memory of that morning – and we went on to spend the whole idle day together until she laughingly and firmly returned my first hesitant kiss; and it was she who silenced my even more fumbled offer of marriage several weeks later. 'No,' she said. 'I don't want to be married. But we can move in together and see how it goes. If it doesn't turn out well we can split and there'll be no bitterness.'

And it was she who found the flat in Hume Street, on the top floor of one of those old Georgian houses in off the Green, within walking distance of both our places of work. There was extraordinary peace and loveliness in those first weeks together that I will always link with those high-ceilinged rooms – the eager rush of excitement I felt as I left the office at the end of the day; the lingering in the streets to buy some offering of flowers or fruit or wine or a bowl and once one copper pan; and then rushing up the stairs to call her name, the emptiness of those same rooms when I'd find she hadn't got home yet.

'Why are we so happy?' I would ask.

'Don't worry it,' she always said, and sealed my lips with a touch.

That early summer we drove down one weekend to the small town in Kilkenny where she had grown up, and above her father's bakery we slept in separate rooms. That Sunday a whole stream of relatives – aunts, cousins, two uncles, with trains of children – kept arriving at the house. Word had gone out, and they had plainly come to look me over. This brought the tension between herself and her schoolteacher mother into open quarrel late that evening after dinner. Her father sat with me in the front room, cautiously kind, sipping whiskey as we measured each careful cliché, listening to the quarrel slow and rise and crack in the far-off kitchen. I had found the sense of comfort and space charming for a while, but by the time we left I, too, was beginning to find the small town claustrophobic.

'Unfortunately the best part of these visits is always the leaving,' she said as we drove away. 'After a while away you're lured into thinking that the next time will somehow be different, but it never is.'

'Wait – wait until you see my place. Then you may well think differently. At least your crowd made an effort. And your father is a nice man.'

'And yet you keep going back to the old place?'

'That's true. That's something in my own nature. I have to face that now. It's just easier for me to go back than to cut. That way I don't feel any guilt. I don't feel anything.'

I knew myself too well. There was more caution than any love or charity in my habitual going home. It was unattractive and it had been learned in the bitter school of my ungiving father. I would fall into no guilt, and I was already fast outwearing him. For a time, it seemed, I could outstare the one eye of nature.

I had even waited for love, if love this was; for it was happiness such as I had never known.

'You see, I waited long enough for you,' I said as we drove away from her Kilkenny town. 'I hope I can keep you now.'

'If it wasn't me it would be some other. My mother will never understand that. You might as well say I waited long enough for you.'

The visit we made to my father, some weeks later, quickly turned to disaster far worse than I had at the very worst envisaged. I saw him watch us as I got out of the car to open the iron gate under the yew, but instead of coming out to greet us he withdrew into the shadows of the hallway. It was my stepmother, Rose, who came out to the car when we both got out and were opening the small garden gate. We had to follow her smiles and trills of speech all the way into the kitchen to find my father, who was seated in the car chair, and he did not rise to take our hands.

After a lunch that was silent, in spite of several shuttlecocks of speech Rose tried to keep in the air, he said as he took his hat from the sill, 'I want to ask you about these walnuts,' and I followed him out into the fields. The mock orange was in blossom, and it was where the mock orange stood out from the clump of egg bushes that he turned suddenly and said, 'What age is your intended? She looks well on her way to forty.'

'She's the same age as I am,' I said blankly. I could hardly think, caught between the shock and pure amazement.

'I don't believe it,' he said.

'You don't have to, but we were in the same class at university.' I turned away.

Walking with her in the same field close to the mock orange tree late that evening, I said, 'Do you know what my father said to me?'

'No,' she said happily. 'But from what I've seen I don't think anything will surprise me.'

'We were walking just here,' I began, and repeated what he'd said. When I saw her go still and pale I knew I should not have spoken.

'He said I look close to forty,' she repeated. 'I have to get out of this place.'

'Stay this one night,' I begged. 'It's late now. We'd have to stay in a hotel. It'd be making it into too big of a production. You don't ever have to come back again, if you don't want to, but stay the night. It'll be easier.'

'I'll not want to come back,' she said as she agreed to see out this one night.

'But why do you think he said it?' I asked her later when we were both quiet, sitting on a wall at the end of the Big Meadow, watching the shadows of the evening deepen between the beeches, putting off the time when we'd have to go into the house, not unlike two grown children.

'Is there any doubt? Out of simple hatred. There's no living with that kind of hatred.'

'We'll leave first thing in the morning,' I promised.

'And why did you', she asked, tickling my throat with a blade of ryegrass, 'say I was, if anything, too beautiful?'

'Because it's true. It makes you public and it's harder to live naturally. You live in too many eyes – in envy or confusion or even simple admiration, it's all the same. I think it makes it harder to live luckily.'

'But it gives you many advantages.'

'If you make use of those advantages, you're drawn even deeper in. And of course I'm afraid it'll attract people who'll try to steal you from me.'

'That won't happen.' She laughed. She'd recovered all her natural good spirits. 'And now I suppose we better go in and face the ogre. We have to do it sooner or later and it's getting chilly.'

My father tried to be very charming when we went in, but there was a false heartiness in the voice that made clear that it grew out of no well-meaning. He felt he'd lost ground, and was now trying to recover it far too quickly. Using silence and politeness like a single weapon, we refused to be drawn in; and when pressed to stay the next morning, we said unequivocally that we had to get back. Except for one summer when I went to

work in England, the summer my father married Rose, I had
always gone home to help at the hay; and after I entered the civil
service I was able to arrange holidays so that they fell around
haytime. They had come to depend on me, and I liked the work.
My father had never forgiven me for taking my chance to go to
university. He had wanted me to stay at home to work the land.
I had always fought his need to turn my refusal into betrayal.
And by going home each summer I felt I was affirming that the
great betrayal was not mine but nature's own.

I had arranged the holidays to fall at haytime that year as I had
all the years before I met her, but since he'd turned to me at the
mock orange tree I was no longer sure I had to go. I was no
longer free, since in everything but name our life together
seemed growing into marriage. It might even make him happy
for a time if he could call it my betrayal.

'I don't know what to do,' I confessed to her a week before I
was due to take holidays. 'They've come to depend on me for
the hay. Everything else they can manage themselves. I know
they'll expect me.'

'What do you want to do?'

'I suppose I'd prefer to go home – that's if you don't mind.'

'Why do you prefer?'

'I like working at the hay. You come back to the city feeling fit
and well.'

'Is that the real reason?'

'No. It's something that might even be called sinister. I've
gone home for so long that I'd like to see it through. I don't want
to be blamed for finishing it, though it'll finish soon, with or
without me. But this way I don't have to think about it.'

'Maybe it would be kinder, then, to do just that, and take the
blame.'

'It probably would be kinder, but kindness died between us
so long ago that it doesn't enter into it.'

'So there was some kindness?'

'When I was younger,' I had to smile. 'He looked on it as
weakness. I suspect he couldn't deal with it. Anyhow it always
redoubled his fury. He was kind, too, in fits, when he was
feeling good about things. That was even more unacceptable.
And that phrase from the Bible is true that after enough

suffering a kind of iron enters the soul. It's very far from commendable, but now I do want to see it through.'

'Well, then go,' she said. 'I don't understand it but I can see you want to go. Being new, the earliest I can get holidays will be September.'

We had pasta and two bottles of red wine at the flat the evening before I was to leave for the hay, and with talking we were almost late for our walk in the Green. We liked to walk there every good evening before turning home for the night.

The bells were fairly clamouring from all corners, rooting vagrants and lovers from the shrubbery, as we passed through the half-closed gates. Two women at the pond's edge were hurriedly feeding the ducks bread from a plastic bag. We crossed the bridge where the Japanese cherry leaned, down among the empty benches round the paths and flowerbeds within their low railings. The deckchairs had been gathered in, the sprinklers turned off. There was about the Green always at this hour some of the melancholy of the beach at the close of holiday. The gate we had entered was already locked. The attendant was rattling an enormous bunch of keys at the one through which we had to leave.

'You know,' she said, 'I'd like to be married before long. I hadn't thought it would make much difference to me, but, oddly, now I want to be married.'

'I hope it's to me,' I said.

'You haven't asked me.'

I could feel her laughter as she held my arm close.

'I'm asking now.'

I made a flourish of removing a non-existent hat. 'Will you marry me?'

'I will.'

'When?'

'Before the year is out.'

'Would you like to go for a drink to celebrate, then?'

'I always like any excuse to celebrate.' She was biting her lip. 'Where will you take me?'

'The Shelbourne. It's our local. It'll be quiet.'

I thought of the aggressive boot thrown after the bridal car, the marbles suddenly rattling in the hub caps of the honeymoon car, the metal smeared with oil so that the thrown boxes of

confetti would stick, the legs of the comic pyjamas hilariously
sewn up. We would avoid all that. We had promised one
another the simplest wedding.

'We live in a lucky time,' she said and raised her glass, her
calm, grey, intelligent eyes shining. 'We wouldn't have been
allowed to do it this way even a decade ago. Will you tell your
father that we're to be married?'

'I don't know. Probably not unless it comes up. And you?'

'I'd better. As it is, Mother will probably be furious that it is
not going to be a big splash.'

'I'm so grateful for these months together. That we were able
to drift into marriage without that drowning plunge when you
see your whole life in a flash. What will you do while I'm away?'

'I'll pine,' she teased. 'I might even try to decorate the flat out
of simple desperation. There's a play at the Abbey that I want to
see. There are some good restaurants in the city if I get too
depressed. And in the meantime, have a wonderful time with
your father and poor Rose in the nineteenth century at the
bloody hay.'

'Oh, for the Lord's sake,' I said and rose to leave. Outside she
was still laughing so provocatively that I drew her towards me.

The next morning on the train home I heard a transistor far
down the carriage promise a prolonged spell of good weather.
Meadows were being mowed all along the line, and I saw men
testing handfuls of hay in the breeze as they waited for the sun
to burn the dew off the fallen swards. It was weather people
prayed for at this time.

I walked the three miles from the station. Meadows were
down all along the road, some already saved, in stacked bales.
The scent of cut grass was everywhere. As I drew close to the
stone house in its trees I could hardly wait to see if the Big
Meadow was down beyond the row of beech trees. When I lived
here I'd felt this same excitement as the train rattled across the
bridges into the city or when I approached the first sight of the
ocean. Now that I lived in a city on the sea the excitement had
been gradually transferred home.

Before I reached the gate I could tell by the emptiness beyond
the beeches that the Big Meadow had been cut. Rose and my
father were in the house. They were waiting in high excitement.

'Everything's ready for you,' Rose said as she shook my hand,

and through the window I saw my old clothes outside in the sun draped across the back of a chair.

'As soon as you get a bite you can jump in your old duds,' my father said. 'I knocked the Big Meadow yesterday. All's ready for go.'

Rose had washed my old clothes before hanging them outside to air. When I changed into them they were still warm from the sun, and they had that lovely clean feel that worn clothes after washing have. Within an hour we were working the machines.

The machines had taken much of the uncertainty and slavery from haymaking, but there was still the anxiety of rain. Each cloud that drifted into the blue above us we watched as apprehensively across the sky as if it were an enemy ship, and we seemed as tired at the end of every day as we were before we had the machines, eating late in silence, waking from listless watching of the television only when the weather forecast showed; and afterwards it was an effort to drag feet to our rooms where the bed lit with moonlight showed like heaven, and sleep was as instant as it was dreamless.

And it was into the stupor of such an evening that the gold watch fell. We were slumped in front of the television set. Rose had been working outside in the front garden, came in and put the tea kettle on the ring, and started to take folded sheets from the linen closet. Without warning, the gold watch spilled out on to the floor. She'd pulled it from the closet with one of the sheets. The pale face was upwards in the poor light. I bent to pick it up. The glass had not broken. 'It's lucky it no longer goes,' Rose breathed.

'Well, if it did you'd soon take good care of that.' My father rose angrily from the rocking chair.

'It just pulled out with the sheets,' Rose said. 'I was running into it everywhere round the house. I put it in with the sheets so that it'd be out of the way.'

'I'm sure you had it well planned. Give us this day our daily crash. Tell me this: would you sleep at night if you didn't manage to smash or break something during the day?' He'd been frightened out of light sleep in the chair. He was intent on avenging his fright.

'Why did the watch stop?' I asked.

I turned the cold gold in my hand. *Elgin* was the one word on the white face. The delicate hands were of blue steel. All through my childhood it had shone.

'Can there be two reasons why it stopped?' His anger veered towards me now. 'It stopped because it got broke.'

'Why can't it be fixed?' I ignored the anger.

'Poor Taylor in the town doesn't take in watches anymore,' Rose answered. 'And the last time it stopped we sent it to Sligo. Sligo even sent it to Dublin but it was sent back. A part that holds the balance wheel is broke. What they told us is, that they've stopped making parts for those watches. They have to be specially handmade. They said that the quality of the gold wasn't high enough to justify that expense. That it was only gold plated. I don't suppose it'll ever go again. I put it in with the sheets to have it out of the way. I was running into it everywhere.'

'Well, if it wasn't fixed before, you must certainly have fixed it for good and forever this time.' My father would not let go.

His hand trembled on the arm of the rocking chair, the same hand that would draw out the gold watch long ago as the first strokes of the Angelus came to us over the heather and pale wheaten sedge of Gloria Bog: 'Twenty minutes late, no more than usual. . . . One of these years Jimmy Lynch will startle himself and the whole countryside by ringing the Angelus at exactly twelve. . . . Only in Ireland is there right time and wrong time. In other countries there is just time.' We'd stand and stretch our backs, aching from scattering the turf, and wait for him to lift his straw hat.

Waiting with him under the yew, suitcases round our feet, for the bus that took us each year to the sea at Strandhill after the hay was in and the turf home; and to quiet us he'd take the watch out and let it lie in his open palm, where we'd follow the small second hand low down on the face endlessly circling until the bus came into sight at the top of Doherty's Hill. How clearly everything sang now set free by the distance of the years, with what heaviness the actual scenes and days had weighed.

'If the watch isn't going to be fixed, then, I might as well have it.' I was amazed at the calm sound of my own words. The watch had come to him from his father. Through all the long years of childhood I had assumed that one day he would pass it on to me. Then all weakness would be gone. I would possess its power. Once in a generous fit he even promised it to me, but he did not keep that promise. Unfairly, perhaps, I expected him to give it to me when I graduated, when I passed into the civil service, when I won my first promotion, but he did not. I had forgotten about it until it had spilled out of the folded sheets on to the floor.

I saw a look pass between my father and stepmother before he said, 'What good would it be to you?'

'No good. Just a keepsake. I'll get you a good new watch in its place. I often see watches in the duty-free airports.' My work often took me outside the country.

'I don't need a watch,' he said, and pulled himself up from his chair.

Rose cast me a furtive look, much the same look that had passed a few moments before between her and my father. 'Maybe your father wants to keep the watch,' it pleaded, but I ignored it.

'Didn't the watch once belong to your father?' I asked as he shuffled toward his room, but the only answer he made was to turn and yawn back before continuing the slow, exaggerated shuffle toward his room.

When the train pulled into Amiens Street Station, to my delight I saw her outside the ticket barrier, in the same tweed suit she'd worn the Saturday morning we met in Grafton Street. I could tell that she'd been to the hairdresser, but there were specks of white paint on her hands.

'Did you tell them that we're to be married?' she asked as we left the station.

'No.'

'Why not?'

'It never came up. And you, did you write home?'

'No. In fact, I drove down last weekend and told them.'

'How did they take it?'

'They seemed glad. You seemed to have made a good impression.' She smiled. 'As I guessed, Mother is quite annoyed that it's not going to be a big do.'

'You won't change our plans because of that.'

'Of course not. She's not much given to change herself, except to changing other people so that they fit in with her ideas.'

'This fell my way at last,' I said and showed her the silent watch. 'I've always wanted it. If we believed in signs it would seem life is falling into our hands at last.'

'And not before our time, I think I can risk adding.'

We were married that October by a Franciscan in their church on the quay, with two vergers as witnesses, and we drank far too much wine at lunch afterwards in a new restaurant that had opened in Lincoln Court; staggering home in the late afternoon, I saw some people in the street smile at my attempt to lift her across the step. We did not even hear the bells closing the Green.

It was dark when we woke, and she said, 'I have something for you,' taking a small, wrapped package from the bedside table.

'You know we promised not to give presents,' I said.

'I know but this is different. Open it. Anyhow, you said you didn't believe in signs.'

It was the gold watch. I held it to my ear. It was running perfectly. The small second hand was circling endlessly low down on the face. The blue hands pointed to past midnight.

'Did it cost much?'

'No. Very little, but that's not your business.'

'I thought the parts had to be specially made.'

'That wasn't true. They probably never even asked.'

'You shouldn't have bothered.'

'Now I'm hoping to see you wear it,' she laughed.

I did not wear it. I left it on the mantel. The gold and white face and delicate blue hands looked very beautiful to me on the white marble. It gave me a curious pleasure mixed with guilt to wind it and watch it run; and the following spring, coming from a conference in Ottawa, I bought an expensive modern watch in the duty-free shop of Montreal Airport. It was guaranteed for five years, and was shockproof, dustproof, waterproof.

'What do you think of it?' I asked her when I returned to Dublin. 'I bought it for my father.'

'Well, it's no beauty, but my mother would certainly approve of it. It's what she'd describe as *serviceable*.'

'It was expensive enough.'

'It looks expensive. You'll bring it when you go down for the hay?'

'It'll probably be my last summer with them at the hay,' I said apologetically. 'Won't you change your mind and come down with me?'

She shook her head. 'He'd probably say I look fifty now.' She was as strong-willed as the schoolteacher mother she disliked, and I did not press. She was with child and looked calm and lovely.

'What'll they do about the hay when they no longer have you to help them?' she said.

'What does anybody do? Do without me. Stop. Get it done by contract. They have plenty of money. It'll just be the end of something that has gone on for a very long time.'

'That it certainly has.'

I came by train at the same time in July as I'd come every summer, the excitement I'd always felt tainted with melancholy that it'd probably be the last summer I would come. I had not even a wish to see it to its natural end anymore. I had come because it seemed less violent to come than to stay away, and I had the good new modern watch to hand over in place of the old gold. The night before, at dinner, we had talked about buying a house with a garden out near the strand in Sandymount. Any melancholy I was feeling lasted only until I came in sight of the house.

All the meadows had been cut and saved, the bales stacked in groups of five or six and roofed with green grass. The Big Meadow beyond the beeches was completely clean, the bales having been taken in. Though I had come intending to make it my last summer at the hay, I now felt a keen outrage that it had been ended without me. Rose and my father were nowhere to be seen.

'What happened?' I asked when I found them at last, weeding the potato ridge one side of the orchard.

'The winter feeding got too much for us,' my father said. 'We decided to let the meadows. Gillespie took them. He cut early – two weeks ago.'

'Why didn't you tell me?'

My father and Rose exchanged looks, and my father spoke as if he was delivering a prepared statement.

'We didn't like to. And anyhow we thought you'd want to come, hay or no hay. It's more normal to come for a rest instead of just to kill yourself at the old hay. And indeed there's plenty else for you to do if you have a mind to do it. I've taken up the garden again myself.'

'Anyhow, I've brought these,' I handed Rose the box of chocolates and bottle of scent, and gave my father the watch.

'What's this for?' He had always disliked receiving presents.

'It's the watch I told you I'd get in place of the old watch.'

'I don't need a watch.'

'I got it anyhow. What do you think of it?'

'It's ugly,' he said, turning it over.

'It was expensive enough.' I named the price. 'And that was duty free.'

'They must have seen you coming, then.'

'No. It's guaranteed for five years. It's dustproof, shockproof, waterproof.'

'The old gold watch – do you still have that?' He changed after silence.

'Of course.'

'Did you ever get it working?'

'No,' I lied. 'But it's sort of nice to have.'

'That doesn't make much sense to me.'

'Well, you'll find that the new watch is working well anyway.'

'What use have I for time here anymore?' he said, but I saw him start to wind and examine the new watch, and he was wearing it at breakfast the next morning. He seemed to want it to be seen as he buttered toast and reached across for milk and sugar.

'What did you want to get up so early for?' he said to me. 'You should have lain in and taken a good rest when you had the chance.'

'What will you be doing today?' I asked.

'Not much. A bit of fooling around. I might get spray ready for the potatoes.'

'It'd be an ideal day for hay,' I said, looking out the window on the fields. The morning was as blue and cool as the plums still touched with dew down by the hayshed. There was a white spider webbing over the grass. I took a book and headed towards the shelter of the beeches in the Big Meadow, for, when the sun would eventually beat through, the day would be uncomfortably hot.

It was a poor attempt at reading. Halfway down each page I'd find I had lost every thread and was staring blankly at the words. I thought at first that the trees and green and those few wisps of cloud, hazy and calm in the emerging blue, brought the tension of past exams and summers too close to the book I held in my hand, but then I found myself stirring uncomfortably in my suit – missing my old loose clothes, the smell of diesel in the meadow, the blades of grass shivering as they fell, the long teeth of the raker kicking the hay into rows, all the jangle and bustle and busyness of the meadows.

I heard the clear blows of a hammer on stone. My father was sledging stones that had fallen from the archway where once the workmen's bell had hung. Some of the stones had been part of the arch and were quite beautiful. There seemed no point in breaking them up. I moved closer, taking care to stay hidden in the shade of the beeches.

As the sledge rose, the watch glittered on my father's wrist. I followed it down, saw the shudder that ran through his arms as the metal met the stone. A watch was always removed from the wrist before such violent work. I waited. In this heat he could not keep up such work for long. He brought the sledge down again and again, the watch glittering, the shock shuddering through his arms. When he stopped, before he wiped the sweat away, he put the watch to his ear and listened intently. What I'd guessed was certain now. From the irritable way he threw the sledge aside, it was clear that the watch was still running.

That afternoon I helped him fill the tar barrel with water for spraying the potatoes, though he made it clear he didn't want help. When he put the bag of blue stone into the barrel to steep, he thrust the watch deep into the water before my eyes.

'I'm going back to Dublin tomorrow,' I said.

'I thought you were coming for two weeks. You always stayed two weeks before.'

'There's no need for me now.'

'It's your holidays now. You're as well off here as by the sea. It's as much of a change and far cheaper.'

'I meant to tell you before, and should have but didn't. I am married now.'

'Tell me more news,' he said with an attempt at cool surprise, but I saw by his eyes that he already knew. 'We heard but we didn't like to believe it. It's a bit late in the day for formal engagements, never mind invitations. I suppose we weren't important enough to be invited.'

'There was no one at the wedding but ourselves. We invited no one, neither her people or mine.'

'Well, I suppose it was cheaper that way,' he agreed sarcastically.

'When will you spray?'

'I'll spray tomorrow,' he said, and we left the blue stone to steep in the barrel of water.

With relief, I noticed he was no longer wearing the watch, but the feeling of unease was so great in the house that after dinner I went outside. It was a perfect moonlit night, the empty fields and beech trees and walls in clear yellow outline. The night seemed so full of serenity that it brought the very ache of longing for all of life to reflect its moonlit calm: but I knew too well it neither was nor could be. It was a dream of death.

I went idly toward the orchard, and as I passed the tar barrel I saw a thin fishing line hanging from a part of the low yew branch down into the barrel. I heard the ticking even before the wrist watch came up tied to the end of the line. What shocked me was that I felt neither surprise nor shock.

I felt the bag that we'd left to steep earlier in the water. The blue stone had all melted down. It was a barrel of pure poison, ready for spraying.

I listened to the ticking of the watch on the end of the line in silence before letting it drop back into the barrel. The poison had already eaten into the casing of the watch. The shining rim and back were no longer smooth. It could hardly run much past morning.

The night was so still that the shadows of the beeches did not waver on the moonlit grass, seemed fixed like a leaf in rock. On the white marble the gold watch must now be lying face upwards in this same light, silent or running. The ticking of the watch down in the barrel was so completely muffled by the spray that only by imagination could it be heard. A bird moved in some high branch, but afterward the silence was so deep it began to hurt, and the longing grew for the bird or anything to stir again.

I stood in that moonlit silence as if waiting for some word or truth, but none came, none ever came; and I grew amused at

that part of myself that still expected something, standing like a
fool out there in all that moonlit silence, when only what *was*
increased or diminished as it changed, became only what is,
becoming again what *was* even faster than the small second
hand endlessly circling in the poison.

Suddenly, the lights in the house went out. Rose had gone to
join my father in bed. Before going into the house this last night
to my room, I drew the watch up again out of the barrel by the
line and listened to it tick, now purely amused by the
expectation it renewed – that if I continued to listen to the
ticking some word or truth might come. And when I finally
lowered the watch back down into the poison, I did it so
carefully that no ripple or splash disturbed the quiet, and time,
hardly surprisingly, was still running; time that did not have to
run to any conclusion.

The Conversion of William Kirkwood

There might well have been no other room in the big stone house but the kitchen, as the rain beat on the slates and windows, swirled about the yard outside. Dampened coats were laid against the foot of the back door, and the panelled oak door that led to the rest of the house was locked because of the faulty handle, the heavy key in the lock. A wood fire flickered in the open door of the huge old range which was freshly black-leaded, its brass fittings gleaming; and beside it Annie May Moran, servant to the Kirkwoods since she was fourteen, sat knitting a brown jersey for her daughter, occasionally bending down to feed logs to the range from a cane basket by her side. At the corner of the long deal table closest to the fire, William Kirkwood sat with her daughter Lucy, helping the child with school exercises. They were struggling more with one another than with algebra, the girl resisting every enticement to understand the use of symbols, but the man was endlessly patient. He spread coins out on the table, then an array of fresh walnuts, and finally took green cooking apples from a bucket. Each time he moved the coins, the nuts, the apples into separate piles she watched him with the utmost suspicion, but was forced each time into giving the correct answer to the simple subtraction by being made to count; but once he substituted x and y for the coins and fruit no number of demonstrations could elicit an answer, and when pressed she avoided understanding with wild guesses.

'You are just being stubborn, Lucy. Sticking your heels in, as usual,' he was forced at length to concede to her.

'It's all right for you, but I'm no good at maths,' she responded angrily.

'It's not that you're no good. It's that you don't want to understand. I don't know what's wrong with you. It seems almost a perversity.'

'I can't understand.'

'Now Lucy. You can't talk to Master William like that,' Annie May said. She still called him Master William though he was now forty-five and last of the Kirkwoods.

'It's all right, Annie May. It'd be worth it all if we could get her to understand. She refuses to understand.'

'It's all right for you to say that, Master William,' Lucy laughed.

'Now, what's next?' he hurried her, 'English and church history?'

'English and catechism notes for tomorrow,' she corrected.

English she loved, and they raced through the exercises. She was tall and strong for her thirteen years and had boyish good looks. When they came to the doctrinal notes, it was plain that he was taking more interest in the exercises than the pupil. Through helping Lucy with these exercises in the evenings, he had first become interested in the Catholic Church. In a way, that had been the first step to his impending conversion. He smiled with pure affection on the girl as she tidied all her books into her leather satchel, and after the three had tea and buttered bread together she came into his arms to kiss him goodnight with the same naturalness as on every night since she had been a small child and he had read her stories. When Annie May unlocked the panelled door, a rush of cold met them from the rest of the house, and she hurried to take the hot water jar and the lighted candle in its blue tin holder to show the child to her upstairs room.

After Eddie Mac, herdsman to the Kirkwoods, as his father had been herdsman before that, had sold the pick of the Kirkwood cattle on the Green in Boyle and disappeared into England with the money, leaving Annie May pregnant, it was old William, William Kirkwood's father, who persuaded Annie May to stay and have the child in the house.

'Why should you have to go to England where you'll know nobody? You did no wrong. Stay and have the child here. We don't have to care what people think. We'll be glad of the child.'

Annie May never once thought of calling the girl by her own name, and she was named Lucy after a favourite aunt of the Kirkwoods. The girl grew strong and healthy, with her father's

dark hair. She loved to shout in the big empty rooms of the
stone house and to laugh with hands on hips as her voice was
echoed back, the laugh then echoing hollowly again, voice and
laugh closer to the clipped commanding accents of the Kirkwoods than to her mother's soft obscured speech, vowel
melting into vowel. The old man and child were inseparable.
Every good day they could be seen together going down to the
orchard to look at the bees, she, clattering away like an alarmed
bird, trying to hold his hand and hop on one foot at the same
time, he, slow by her side, inscrutable behind the beekeeper's
veil. And it was Lucy he sent to find William that final day when
he wasn't able to lift the tops of the hives, imagining that they
had all been stuck down by the bees. It was a sunny spring day.
The bees were making cleansing flights from the hives.

'I can't understand it, William,' the beekeeper explained to his
son when Lucy brought him to the hives.

'If the bees have stuck the roofs down, Father, we may need a
hive tool. I'll try to twist them and ease them up slowly,'
William said, but found to his consternation that the roof was
loose in his hands and lifted easily. 'They're not stuck at all.
They're quite free.' He began to laugh, only to fall into amazed
silence when he saw that his father had grown too weak to lift
the few boards of painted pine. Gently he led the old man and
puzzled child back to the house.

'You must have caught something, Father. A few days in bed
and you'll be fine.'

During that same windless spring night in which a light rain
fell around the big house and its trees like a veil, the old
beekeeper sank steadily, and near morning slipped as gently out
of life as he had passed through.

Annie May wept bitterly for the old man, but Lucy was too
young for grief and turned naturally to William. She started to
go with him everywhere, about the sheds and out into the
fields. She was as good as any boy at driving sheep and cattle.
Annie May tried to put some curb on these travels, but Lucy was
headstrong and hated housework. Besides, not only did William
seem to like the girl's company in the fields but he often found
her extremely useful. It was as a gesture of some recompense to
Annie May for stealing the child's hours in the fields – as well as
that of a naturally pedagogic nature – that led him to help Lucy

from her early years with her school exercises in the winter evenings.

Except for his isolation with Annie May and Lucy in the stone house, the war found William Kirkwood little better off than his Catholic neighbours, poorer than some Catholics already on the rise. He had a drawing-room and library and lawn and orchard and spreading fields within stone walls: but the lawn was like a meadow; many of the books on the high shelves of the library had been damaged by the damp; the orchard was wild, his father's beehives rotting away unseen in the high grass at its foot; the many acres had been understocked and half-farmed for too long, and there were broken gaps in the stone walls. Nearly all the other Protestant landowners, friends of his parents, presences in his youth, seeing the erosion of their old ascendancy, had emigrated to Canada, Australia, or moved to the North. William Kirkwood stayed, blessedly unaware that he had become a mild figure of fun, out watching the stars at night as a young man when he should have been partying with the Protestant blades or parading their confident women among the prize floral arrangements and cattle and horses and sheaves of barley of the shows; now struggling on miles of good land to support himself, an old servant woman and her illegitimate child. But this laughter was based on no knowledge of the man. It came from casual observation, complacent ignorance, simple prejudice, that lazy judgement that comes more easily than any sympathy, and it was to receive a severe jolt because of the war away in Europe. A neutral Ireland declared it *The Emergency*. Local defence forces were formed. William Kirkwood saw no division of loyalty and was among the first to join. He was given a commission, and the whole local view of him – humorous, derisory, patronizing – changed. He proved to be a crack marksman. He could read field maps at a glance.

His mother's father had been old Colonel Darby, half-deaf, with a stiff leg and a devotion to gin, who was not much mentioned around the stone house because he had never let slip a single opportunity to pour sarcasm and insult on his gentle sober son-in-law, William's father. The Darbys had been British officers far back, and once William Kirkwood put on uniform it was as if they gathered to claim him. Men who had joined for the free army boots and uniform, for the three weeks in Finner

Camp by the sea on full pay every summer, got an immediate shock. The clipped commands demanded instant compliance. A cold eye searched out every small disorder of dress or stance or movement. There were mutterings, 'Put one of them back on a horse and it's as if they never left the saddle. They'd ride you down like a dog,' but they had to admit that he was fair, and when he led the rifle team to overall victory in the first Western Shield, and was promoted Captain, Commanding Officer for the north of the county, a predictable pride stirred and slow praise, 'He's not as bad as he appears at first,' began to grow about his name.

Out of uniform he was as withdrawn as before and as useless on land. Lucy was with him everywhere still. Though school and church had softened her accent, it still held more than a hint of the sharp unmistakable Protestant bark, and she took great pride in William's new uniform and rank. She had caused a disturbance at school by taking a stick and driving some boys from the ball alley who had sneered at William's Protestantism: 'He doesn't even go to his own church.'

'He has no church to go to. It was closed,' she responded and took up her stick.

Annie May had lost all control of her, and often William found himself ruling in favour of the mother, caught uncomfortably between them, but mostly Lucy did William's bidding. To be confined with her mother in the house was the one unacceptable punishment. To be with William in the fields was joy. She helped him all that poor wet summer at the hay. She could drive the horse-raker and was more agile than he. Beyond what work she did, and it was considerable, her presence by his side in the field was a deep sustenance. He shuddered to think of facing the long empty fields stretching ahead like heartache, the broken sky above, without her cheerful clatter by his side, her fierce energy.

And it seemed only right that she was by his side on the morning that the long isolation of the Kirkwoods ended.

The hay had been turned in the big rock meadow but rain was promised by evening. What lay ahead of them, even with the help of the horse-raker, was disheartening. They would have to try to save as much as they were able. What still lay on the ground by evening would have to take its chance of better weather. They could do no more.

Suddenly, there was a shout in the meadow, and Francie Harte came swaggering towards them. Francie had given William much trouble in the early days of the Force. He had been forever indulging in practical jokes.

'Is there anything wrong with me dress today, Captain?' he shouted out as he came close. His walk was awkward because of the hayfork hidden behind his back.

'No, Francie. We are not in uniform today,' William Kirkwood replied mildly, not knowing what to make of the apparition. Then a cheer went up from behind the roadside hedge and the whole company of men swarmed into the field. Another man was opening the gate to let in an extra horse and raker. Haycocks started to spring up the field before the shouting, joking, cursing, jostling tide of men. Lucy was sent racing to the house to tell Annie May to start making sandwiches. William himself went to Charlie's for a half-barrel of porter. Long before night the whole field was swept clean. After the men had gone William Kirkwood walked the field, saw all the haycocks raked and tied down.

'That would take you and me most of a week, Lucy, and we'd probably lose half of it,' he said in his reflective way, almost humbly.

The promised rain arrived by evening. Its rhythmic beating on the slates brought him no anxiety. He heard it fall like heartsease and slept.

The same help arrived to bring the hay in from the fields, and they came for the compulsory wheat and root crops as well. Not even in the best years, when they could afford to take on plenty of labour, had the whole work of summer and harvest gone so easily. To return the favours, since none of the men would accept money, William Kirkwood had to go in turn to the other farms. Each time that she wasn't allowed to go with him Lucy was furious and sulked for days. He was no use at heavy labouring work on the farms, and he was never subjected to the cruelty of competition with other men, but he had an under- standing of machinery that sometimes made him more useful than stronger men. As well as by his new military rank, he was protected by the position that the Kirkwoods had held for generations and had never appeared to abuse. He was a novelty in the fields, a source of talk and gossip against the relentless

monotony of the work and days. His strangeness and gentle
manners made him exceedingly popular with the girls and
women, and the distance he always kept, like the unavailability
of a young priest, only increased his attractiveness. After the
years of isolation, he seemed very happy amid all the new bustle
and, for the first time in years, he found that the land was actually
making money. At Christmas he offered Annie May a substantial
sum as a sort of reparation for the meagre pay she had been
receiving, unchanged, for years. This she indignantly refused.

'It was pay enough for me to be let stay on here all these years
without a word. I wouldn't ever want to insult you, but I'll throw
that sort of money on the floor if you force it on me.'

'Well then, we'll take Lucy to the town. She's no longer a child.
She needs a whole new outfit like the other girls.'

'Isn't she all right the way she is? All it'll do is give her notions.
What'll notions do in her place but bring in trouble!'

She would take nothing for herself, but on Lucy she yielded.
They went together to Boles. Annie May had never set foot in
Boles before and she was awed into silence, starting with fright
each time the pulleys sent the brass cups hurtling along the wires
to the cashier in her glass case above in the shop, starting again
each time the cups came crashing back with receipts and change.
With much help from Mrs Boles, and the confused choices of
Lucy, it was William himself who decided the outfit, old Boles all
the time hovering around at the sight of the last of the Kirkwoods.

'I was only that height when I used see your dear mother come
into the shop. Oh, she was a lady,' rubbing his hands, the eternal
red rose in his buttonhole seemingly never affected by winter or
summer.

'You look beautiful, Lucy, but I hate to see you growing up,'
William complimented the girl simply. Lucy blushed and went to
kiss him on the lips, but he found that he was hardly able to lift
her into his arms.

The first Sunday she went to Mass and the rails in this outfit she
created an even greater sensation than did William when he first
stood as just another workman in one of his neighbours' fields.

The war ground on with little effect. The activities of the local
force were now routine: the two weeks in Finner Camp, rifle
competitions, drill on Thursday evenings, rifle practice on Sunday afternoons – firing from the Oakport shore at targets set in

the back of McCabe's Hill. On certain Sunday mornings the
Force assembled in full dress at the Hall, marched through the
village to the church, where they stood on guard in front of the
altar during the sung Mass, presenting arms before and after the
consecration. Captain Kirkwood marched his men through the
village on these Sundays, but at the church door turned over his
command to the schoolteacher, Lieutenant McLoughlin, and
remained outside until Mass had ended. Now that he had
become such a part of the people it was felt that such a pointed
difference was a little sad. This was brought up in bumbling
fashion to William's face by Garda Sergeant Moran in Charlie's
front room or parlour one Sunday after rifle practice. It was
usual for the whole company to go to Charlie's for a drink after
these Sunday practices. The men drank standing up behind the
wooden partition that separated the bar from the grocery, but
the two officers, Captain Kirkwood and Lieutenant McLoughlin, sat with the Garda Sergeant around the big oval table in the
front room. The Sergeant attended these rifle practices to make
sure that certain safety precautions were observed. He had been
drinking after Mass, and had made a nuisance of himself at the
practice, wandering around during firing looking for someone
to talk to, but as he did not come under his command there was
very little Captain Kirkwood could do. As soon as Charlie
brought the whiskeys to the front room, the Sergeant began:
'Before the war, William, you were there on your own in that big
house, helping nobody, getting no help. Now you're in with
everybody. Only for your being a Protestant, there'd not be the
slightest difference now between you and the rest of us. I fear it
takes war to bring people to their senses.'

Lieutenant McLoughlin was searching furiously for some
phrase to stifle the embarrassing speech, a verbal continuation
of the nuisance they had been subjected to all day when William
Kirkwood drily remarked, 'Actually, Sergeant, I'm seriously
considering becoming a Catholic, but not, I'm afraid, in the
interests of conformity,' which brought a stunned silence to the
room which was even more embarrassing than the Sergeant's
speech.

To remark that it was a little sad that such a pointed difference
still stood out was polite weak sentiment; for William Kirkwood
to turn Catholic was alarming. It broke the fierce law that

everybody stayed within the crowd they were born into, like the sparrows or blackbirds. They changed for a few reasons, and for those reasons only, money or position, mostly inseparable anyway, and *love*, if it can be called love when the instinct fastens on one person and will commit any madness to obtain its desire. Catholics had turned Protestant for money or position, it was an old sore and taunt; but the only reason a Protestant was ever known to turn was in order to marry. They had even a living effigy of it within the parish, the Englishman Sinclair, who had married one of the Conways, his poor wife telling the people in Boyle he had gone to Mass in Cootehall, then fibbing to the Cootehall people that he went to Mass in Boyle, when the whole world knew that he was at home toasting his shins and criticizing everything and everybody within sight: 'It was no rush of faith that led to my conversion. I was dragged into your Apostolic Roman Catholic Church by my male member,' he would shout and chuckle.

'How did it come about that *you* got interested . . .?' McLoughlin asked William tentatively.

'Helping Lucy with her school exercises,' William answered readily. 'I became interested in some of the catechism answers, then church history. It's true it is the older church. I found books by Newman and the Oxford Movement in the library. My mother must have been interested once.'

'Still, it must be no joke turning your back on your own crowd, more or less saying that they were wrong all those centuries,' the Sergeant said.

'No. Not if one is convinced of the truth,' William pushed his glass away and rose. 'They lived according to their light. It is our day now.'

'Well, whatever you do, we hope it'll be for the best,' both men echoed as he left. William never took more than one drink and this had always been put down to Protestant abstemiousness.

'That's a lemoner for you. I'll need a good slow pint to get the better of that,' the Sergeant breathed when he had gone, and pressed the bell. They both had pints.

'What's behind it?' the Sergeant demanded.

'I'd not give you many guesses.'

'How?'

'It's fairly plain. I'd give you no more than one guess.'

'You have me beaten.'

'How did he get interested in catholicism?'

'With Lucy and the catechism,' the Sergeant said in amazement. 'I should have seen it sooner. He took her to Boles before Christmas and dressed her like the Queen of Sheba, and she hardly fourteen!'

'In some ways Kirkwood is a very clever masterful man, but in other ways he is half a child. Lucy is not good at school but she's far from stupid and in many ways she's older than her years. She's more a Kirkwood to the bone than the daughter of poor old Annie May. Isn't she with him everywhere?'

'He couldn't marry her though.'

'Three or four years isn't that far away. Wouldn't it leave Annie May sitting pretty!'

'God, I'd never have thought of that in a hundred years.'

The news of the impending conversion was so strange that they kept it to themselves. On reflection they didn't quite believe it and wanted not to appear fools, but when William was seen walking the avenue of young lime trees to the presbytery every Tuesday and Thursday evening for mandatory instruction it became widespread. Miracles would never cease among the stars of heaven. William Kirkwood, last of the Kirkwoods, was about to renounce the error of their ways and become a Catholic.

Canon Glynn, the old priest, was perfectly suited to his place. He had grown up on a farm, was fond of cards and whiskey, but his real passion in life was for the purebred shorthorns he grazed on the church grounds. In public he was given to emphasizing the mercy rather than the wrath of God and in private believed that the affairs of the earth ran more happily the less God was brought into them altogether. At first he found the visits of this odd catechumen a welcome break in his all too predictable evenings, but soon began to be worn out by his pupil's seemingly insatiable appetite for theological speculation. William was now pursuing catholicism with the same zeal he had given for years to astronomy, reading every book on theology and church history he could lay hands on. Rather than be faced with this strenuous analysis of the Council of Trent, the old priest would have much preferred to have poured this over-intellectual childlike man a large glass of whiskey and to have talked about the five purebred shorthorns he was keeping over the winter and which he foddered himself in all weathers before saying daily Mass.

'Look, William. You already know far more about doctrine than any of my parishioners, and I've never seen much good come from all this probing,' he was driven to state one late evening. 'We are human. We cannot know God or Truth. It is shut away from our eyes. We can only accept and believe. It may be no more than the mother's instinct for the child, and as blind, but it is all we have. In two weeks' time, when I'll ask you "Do you believe?" all I want from you is the loud and clear response, "I do." There our part will end. Yours will begin. In my experience anything too much discussed and worried about always leads to staleness.'

William Kirkwood was far from blind. He understood at once that he had tired the old priest whom he had grown to like and respect. For the next two weeks, like the too obedient son he had always been, he was content to sit and follow wherever the priest's conversation led, which, after the second whiskey, was invariably to the five purebred shorthorns now grazing on the short sweet grass that grew above the ruins of the once famous eighth-century monastery.

'You can still see the monks' tracks everywhere in the fields, their main road or street, the cells, what must have been their stables, all like a plan on paper. Of course the walls of the main buildings still stand, but they are much later, twelfth century. Great minds thundered at one another there once. Now my shorthorns take their place. It is all good, William,' he would laugh.

At the end of the period of instruction, when the priest, a mischievous twinkle in his old eyes, asked, 'Do you accept and believe all those revealed truths and mysteries?' William Kirkwood smiled, bowed his head and said, 'I do, Father.'

The next morning, beside the stone font at the back of the Cootehall Church, water was poured over the fine greying head of William Kirkwood. As it trickled down on to the brown flagstones, it must have seemed a final pale bloodletting to any ghosts of the Kirkwoods hovering in the air around.

Annie May and Lieutenant McLoughlin stood as his god-parents. Afterwards there were smiles, handshakes, congratulatory armclasps, and after Mass a big festive breakfast in the presbytery, attended by all the local priests and teachers and prominent parishioners. Annie May and Lucy were there as well. The only flaw in the perfect morning was that Lucy looked pale and tense throughout and on the very verge of tears when having to respond to a few polite questions during the breakfast. She had been strange with William ever since he began instruction, as if she somehow sensed that this change threatened the whole secure world of her girlhood with him. As soon as they got home from the breakfast, she burst into an uncontrollable fit of weeping and ran to her room. By evening she was better but would not explain her weeping, and that night was the first night in years that she did not come to him to be kissed on her way to bed. The following Sunday every eye was on the recent convert as he marched his men through the village and all the way up the church to the foot of the high altar. Lucy felt light-headed with pride as she saw him ascend the church at the head of his men. But the old ease between them had disappeared. She no longer wanted his help in the evenings with her exercises, preferring to go to school unprepared if necessary, and he did not try to force his help, waiting until this mood would pass.

'Now that you have come this far, and everything has gone so well, you might as well go the whole distance,' the Sergeant suggested with amiable vagueness one Sunday soon afterwards in Charlie's. Rifle practice had been abandoned early. A ricochet had somehow come off the hill, had struck a red bullock of Murphy's in the eye in a nearby field. The bullock, lowing wildly, began to stagger in circles round the field. A vet had to put it down. A report would have to be written. The accident had been the first in his command and William Kirkwood was inordinately annoyed. There must have been carelessness or wilful folly somewhere among the riflemen.

'What do you mean?' he asked very sharply.

'It was nothing about today,' McLoughlin interjected. 'I think the Sergeant was only trying to say what we all feel. Everything has gone wonderfully well and it would complete the picture if we were to see you married,' and both men saw William Kirkwood suddenly colour to the roots of his hair.

'I'm too old,' he said.

'You left it late but it's certainly far from too late.'

The conversation had brought on so much confusion that it was let drop. William left as usual after the one whiskey.

'I'm afraid you struck the mark there,' McLoughlin said as soon as they were alone.

'How?'

'You said what was plainly on his mind.'

'It's hardly Lucy.'

'Lucy's not in it at this stage, though she's upset at school enough about something or other,' the teacher said.

'What are we to do, then? We can't just go out and find any old bird for the last of the Kirkwoods. She'll have to be able to flap at least one good wing.'

'I suppose you'll be changing to pints now,' Charlie appeared at the doorway, and without waiting for an answer, went and cleared the whiskey glasses from the table.

'A pair of pints, Charlie,' the Sergeant said exuberantly. 'Nothing decent ever stands alone. How long is it since we bundled you into the car that Sunday and found your good woman for you?'

'It must be the best part of five years, Sergeant,' Charlie laughed defensively, and when he laughed the tip of his small red nose wrinkled upwards in a curl.

'It was a drastic solution to a drastic problem. You had the place nearly drunk out after your mother died. The first six women we called on that Sunday turned us down flat.'

'I doubt they did right. I was no great catch.'

'We were about to give up for that Sunday when we called on Baby. She said before we finished, "I'll take him. I know the bar and the farm," and we brought you in out of the car.'

'Maybe that's when she made her big mistake,' Charlie tried to joke.

'She made no mistake,' the teacher put in gently, afraid that Charlie was being hurt by the Sergeant's egotism, oblivious of everything but his own part in that Sunday. 'She made the best move of her life. Look where you both are today – children, money. Who could want more?'

'Maybe it's as good as the other thing anyhow.' Charlie laughed with unchanged defensiveness.

'It's far better. This love business we hear so much about nowadays is a pure washout,' the teacher said definitively.

'One thing is sure,' the Sergeant said after Charlie had brought them the pints. 'We can't bundle William Kirkwood into the back of a car and drive *him* around for a whole Sunday until we find him a wife,' and at the very absurdity of the picture both men began to laugh until tears ran from their eyes, and they had to pound their glasses on the table. When they were quiet, the Sergeant said, 'There are more ways of choking a dog than with butter,' which renewed the laughter.

What they didn't know was that Charlie had been standing in the hallway all the time, rigid with anger as he listened. 'The pair of bitches,' he said quietly, his anger calming as he moved to face the men who were growing rowdy behind the wooden partition.

'What will we do about the Captain? He didn't seem averse to the idea,' the Sergeant was saying in the parlour.

'We can't, as you put it, bring in any old bird. We'll have to look hard and carefully. It'd be a very nice thing to see the Captain married.' The teacher was serious.

The first to be approached was Eileen Casey, the junior mistress in the school in Keadue. She was twenty-eight, small, with very blonde straight hair, fond of reading, pretty in a withdrawn way. Her headmaster, a friend of McLoughlin's, brought it up over the tea and sandwiches of the school lunch hour. When it was clear that she was not interested and was going out with a boy from her own place near Killala and was looking for a school closer to home so that they could marry, he pretended it had been nothing but a joke on his part. 'We like to see how these rich converts look in our girls' eyes.'

After this, the Sergeant and McLoughlin sat for a whole evening and compiled a list of girls. They were true to their word that they couldn't bring in just any old bird. All the girls they picked were local flowers, and they knew they faced the probability of many rebuffs, but they studied how to go about it as circuitously and discreetly as possible.

Before this got under way, William Kirkwood came to McLoughlin's bungalow to dinner for the first time. He felt ill at ease in the low rooms, the general cosiness, the sweet wine in cut glasses, and Mrs McLoughlin's attempts at polite conversation. Not in all the years of his Protestantism had he ever felt his difference so keenly, and what struck him most was the absence of books in a schoolmaster's house. He disliked spirits after dinner, but this evening he was glad of the glass of whiskey in his hand as he faced McLoughlin in his front room while Mrs McLoughlin did the washing up. Around him, among the religious pictures and small statues, were all the heirlooms and photos of a married life that seemed to advance with resolute cheerfulness towards some sought-after stereotype. He was on edge, and when McLoughlin said, 'We've started looking,' he practically barked, 'For what?'

'For a good woman for you,' McLoughlin didn't notice the edge and smiled sweetly.

'Dear Peter . . . I had no idea . . . This is too ridiculous,' William Kirkwood was on his feet at once. 'It is positively antediluvian,' he had started to laugh dangerously. 'Fortunately, no one will have me. Imagine the embarrassment of some poor woman who was fool enough to have me when she found I couldn't abide her! I'd have to marry her. You couldn't do otherwise to any unfortunate two-legged.'

McLoughlin sat the outburst through in open-mouthed dismay. 'We thought you'd like to be married.'

'That's true. I would.'

He was even further taken aback by the positiveness of the ready response. 'Is there any person you had in mind yourself?' McLoughlin was glad to find any words on his lips.

'Yes. There is,' came even more readily still. 'But what's the use? She'd never have me.'

'May I ask who she is?'

'Of course you can. I was thinking of Miss Kennedy. Mary Kennedy.'

'Well then. I don't see why you had to get in such a state,' it was McLoughlin's turn to attack. 'She was the first girl we were thinking of approaching.'

McLoughlin was not so much surprised by the preference as by the fact that the solitary isolated 'odd' Kirkwood should have a preference at all.

The Kennedys were a large local family, had good rock land and part of the woods, owned a sawmill and a small adjoining factory making crates and huge wooden drums on which electric cable was rolled. They had been rich enough to send Mary and her sisters to the Ursulines in Sligo. There she was nicknamed 'big hips', more for her laughing vitality than measurements. From the Ursulines she went to train as a nurse in the Mater Hospital in Dublin. She was black-haired and tall, too sharp featured to be beautiful, but there was about her an excitement and vitality that was more than beauty. Even the way she had of scratching her head as she laughed, her wide stance, intrigued men. At the Mater, she fell in love with a pale young doctor, conscientious and dull, who was flattered at first, but gradually he backed away from her high spirits. When he broke with her, she came home, where she hung listlessly about the house for six months, sometimes going for long solitary walks.

It was on one of those walks that William Kirkwood met her in his own fields. She had been surprised by a play of the late October light all the way across the top of the hill, and there being no purpose to her walk she had crossed the stone wall to follow that streak of evening along the hill. To William's polite enquiry, 'May I help you in any way, Miss Kennedy?' she had responded with a certain mischievousness – 'No, thank you, Mr Kirkwood. I'm just out for a walk' – because it was unheard of for a local person to be just out for a walk. Mary Kennedy was surprised to find the 'young Mr Kirkwood' that they used to laugh about when she was a child – the same Mr Kirkwood who spent all fine nights out in the fields studying the stars through a telescope and his days reading or in bed – a middle-aged man, tall and beautifully mannered certainly, but middle-aged. They chatted for a while before separating. She didn't think much about the meeting but, apart from the good manners, what she remembered most was his openness and the lack of furtiveness; and furtiveness was what she found in most Irish men when faced with a young woman.

She returned to the Mater, but her confidence was broken and she had to school herself to meet the young doctor on the wards or along corridors, to smile and be polite when she felt like hiding or running. She saw with a dull clarity that most women's social position in Ireland was decided for the rest of their lives by one single unfair throw of the dice, and she had too much of the Kennedys' sense of themselves to be interested in the young civil servants, policemen, and prison officers that were available to the other nurses. William Kirkwood felt that *he* should approach Mary Kennedy himself, but he knew too well that if left to his own devices he would think a great deal about it and do nothing.

'How did you propose to approach Miss Kennedy?' he asked McLoughlin.

'We didn't intend to put you into the back of a car and drive you round some fine Sunday anyhow,' McLoughlin was now in the ascendant. 'I know one of her brothers. If she had someone else or wasn't interested, that would be the end of it. The Kennedys do not talk. If on the other hand . . .' McLoughlin spread his hands in a gesture that meant that all things were possible.

Mary Kennedy listened carefully to the proposal her brother brought. She had suffered and was close to the age of reconcilement. The tide was not lingering.

She recalled the meeting in the fields. The few times they had met since then he had smiled and saluted in passing. There was the big stone house in its trees, the walled orchard, the avenue, the lawn, the spreading fields . . . no mean setting.

A boast she had made carelessly once among girls came back to her. Love was not important, she had declared. She would love whichever man she married, whether she loved him or not before they married. This could be tested at last. She told her brother that she would meet William Kirkwood but could promise nothing.

They met in the Wicklow Hotel and had dinner there. She wore a suit of black corduroy with a plain silver necklace and was more at ease than he with the formalities of dinner.

'I was surprised you knew my name the time we met in the fields,' she said.

'That's quite simple. I had admired you and asked your name. But you knew my name then?'

'There was only one Mr Kirkwood. There are many Kennedys,' she smiled back.

When she saw him waiting for her later in the hotel foyer, the well-cut but worn blue pinstripe, the thick, lank grey hair, the jutting Anglo-Irish jaw, the military appearance of alertness, she knew that he was superior to most men she was likely to come on in the city, and she noticed how soft and long his hands were from years of gentle living. The hands of her own brothers were already large and coarse by comparison. They had two other meetings in the city before she agreed to come down and look over the big stone house and its grounds, but she had already made up her mind that she would marry William Kirkwood.

The first sight Annie May had of her the Sunday she came to the house was standing beneath the copper beech on the front avenue. A handbag hung from her shoulder. William Kirkwood was smiling on her. The flurry of the past weeks, the visits to Dublin, the need for ironed shirts and polished shoes fell into place. The pain that filled her chest climbed into a tight band about her forehead. That there was no one to blame; that it was in the natural order of things only made it more painful. She couldn't even be angry.

They came to the big kitchen by way of the front door, looking in on the library and drawing-room, and Annie May heard her admiring the stairs.

'What is this room with all the marble?' she heard her ask as they drew closer.

'It's just a pantry now. In the old days it was the flower-cutting room . . . where the roses were cut.'

When they came through the door, there was nothing but smiles, handshakes, all politeness, but it was extremely tense. If William Kirkwood knew more of human nature, he would have seen that the two women were territorial enemies.

'Where's Lucy?' he asked.

'I don't know. She was here up to a minute ago,' Annie May said and offered to make tea.

'I'd love a cup of tea,' Mary Kennedy said. 'But first I'd like to see the upstairs rooms.'

While they were taking tea, after having spent a long time walking through the upstairs rooms, darkness fell but still there was no sight of Lucy.

'She must have gone outside,' Annie May said worriedly, her own anxiety already transferred to the child.

William Kirkwood walked Mary Kennedy over the fields to the road that led to her house. When they got to the house, it was full of the Kennedys and their families, most of whom William was meeting for the first time. It was a pleasant evening, and by its end it was clear to Mary that both William Kirkwood and the match were approved of. For his part, he liked the big old ramshackle farmhouse, the crowd of people, the lashings of food and whiskey, the natural cheerfulness of people enjoying themselves, the absence of formality and self-consciousness, reminding him more of political celebration than a family evening. When he left, Mary walked with him to the avenue. On the walk she kissed him for the first time. She was planning the wedding for June. The house would have to be painted, new curtains bought, some new furniture chosen. 'The whole house will have to be opened up again. As it stands, the kitchen is the only room that looks lived in.'

As he walked with her, he felt that the night was bathed in a dream of happiness, and would start in disbelief that this tall elegant high-spirited woman was about to become his wife. For her part, she felt that her girlish boast was coming true. She knew that she was going to love this strange man who spoke terms of endearment as if they were commands. 'Venus, Mars, Saturn, Jupiter to the east over there,' he was barking out the names in the clear sky, and she had to bite back laughter. She knew of men much less knowledgeable about the stars who would be able to turn them to better advantage, but she would take care of that in her own time.

'There's one thing more,' she said before they parted. 'Annie May will have to be given notice.'

'That I could never do,' he said with such vehemence that it took her back. 'She came as a very young girl to work for my mother. Lucy was born here, grew up here. I could never tell them to leave.'

When she saw how disturbed he was, she put her hand on his arm. 'Don't worry, love. You'll not have to do anything. I doubt very much if Annie May will want to stay once she hears I am moving into the house in June.'

They were both standing still at the gate, and she turned and raised her lips to his, and he, feeling her body stir against his, took her into his arms.

His own house was in darkness when he got home. He knew the back door was unlocked, but rather than go through the empty kitchen he let himself in by the front door with his key. There he sat for a long time in the cold of the library. He had many things to think about, and not least among them was this: whether there was any way his marriage could take place without bringing suffering on two people who had been a great part of his life, who had done nothing themselves to deserve being driven out into a world they were hardly prepared for.

Bank Holiday

It had been unusual weather, hot for weeks, and the white morning mist above the river, making ghostly the figures crossing the metal bridge, seemed a certain promise that the good weather was going to last beyond the holiday. All week in the Department he had heard the girls talking of going down the country, of the ocean, and the dances in the carnival marquees. Already, across the river, queues were forming for the buses that went to the sea – Howth, Dollymount, Malahide. He, Patrick McDonough, had no plans for the holiday, other than to walk about the city, or maybe to go out into the mountains later. He felt a certain elation of being loose in the morning, as if in space. The solid sound of his walking shoes on the pavement seemed to belong to someone else, to be going elsewhere.

A year ago he had spent this holiday in the country, among the rooms and fields and stone walls he had grown up with, as he had spent it every year going back many years. His mother was still living, his father had died the previous February. The cruellest thing about that last holiday was to watch her come into the house speaking to his father of something she had noticed in the yard – a big bullfinch feeding on the wild strawberries of the bank, rust spreading in the iron of one of the sheds – and then to see her realize in the midst of speech that her old partner of the guaranteed responses was no longer there. They had been close. His father had continued to indulge her once great good looks long after they had disappeared.

That last holiday he had asked his mother to come and live with him in the city, but she had refused without giving it serious thought. 'I'd be only in the way up there. I could never fit in with their ways now.' He had gone down to see her as often as he was able to after that, which was most weekends, and had paid a local woman to look in on her every day. Soon he saw that his visits no longer excited her. She had even lost interest in most of the things around her, and whenever that interest briefly gleamed she turned not to him but to his dead father. When pneumonia took her in a couple of days just before Christmas, and her body was put down beside her husband's in Aughawillian churchyard, he was almost glad. The natural wind now blew directly on him.

He sold the house and lands. The land had been rich enough to send him away to college, not rich enough to bring him back other than on holiday, and now this holiday was the first such in years that he had nowhere in particular to go, no one special to see, nothing much to do. As well as the dangerous elation this sense of freedom gave, he looked on it with some of the cold apprehension of an experiment.

Instead of continuing on down the quays, he crossed to the low granite wall above the river, and stayed a long time staring down through the vaporous mist at the frenzy and filth of the low tide. He could have stood mindlessly there for most of the morning but he pulled himself away and continued on down the quays until he turned into Webb's Bookshop.

The floor in Webb's had been freshly sprinkled and swept, but it was dark within after the river light. He went from stack to stack among the second-hands until he came on a book that caught his interest, and he began to read. He stood there a long time until he was disturbed by the brown-overalled manager speaking by his side.

'Would you be interested in buying the book, sir? We could do something perhaps about the price. The books in this stack have been here a long time.' He held a duster in his hand, some feathers tied round the tip of a cane.

'I was just looking.'

The manager moved away, flicking the feathers along a row of spines in a gesture of annoyance. The spell was ended, but it was fair enough: the shop had to sell books, and he knew that if he bought the book it was unlikely that he would ever give it the same attention again. He moved to the next stack, not wanting to appear driven from the shop. He pretended to inspect other volumes. He lifted and put down *The Wooing of Elisabeth McCrum*, examining other books cursorily, all the time moving towards the door. It was no longer pleasant to remain. He tried

to ignore the manager's stare as he went out, to find himself in
blinding sunshine on the pavement. The mist had completely
lifted. The day was uncomfortably hot. His early excitement and
sense of freedom had disappeared.

Afterwards he was to go over the little incident in the
bookshop. If it had not happened would he have just ventured
again out into the day, found the city too hot for walking, taken
a train to Bray as he thought he might and walked all day in the
mountains until he was dog-tired and hungry? Or was this sort
of let-down the inescapable end of the kind of elation he had felt
walking to the river in the early morning? He would never
know. What he did know was that once outside the bookshop
he no longer felt like going anywhere and he started to retrace
his steps back to where he lived, buying a newspaper on the
way. When he opened the door a telegram was lying on the
floor of the hallway.

It was signed 'Mary Kelleher', a name he didn't know. It
seemed that a very old friend, James White, who worked for the
Tourist Board in New York, had given her his name. There was
a number to call.

He put it aside to sit and read through the newspaper, but he
knew by the continuing awareness of the telegram on the table
that he would call. He was now too restless to want to remain
alone.

James White and he had met when they were both young civil
servants, White slightly the older – though they both seemed
the same age now – the better read, the more forthright, the
more sociable. They met at eight-thirty on the Friday night of
every week for several years, the evening interrupted only by
holidays and illnesses, proof against girlfriends, and later wives,
ended only by White's transfer abroad. They met in bars,
changing only when they became known to the barmen or
regulars, and in danger of losing their anonymity. They talked
about ideas, books, 'the human situation', and 'reality and
consciousness' often surfaced with the second or third pint.
Now he could hardly remember a sentence from those hundreds of evenings. What he did remember was a barman's face,
white hair drawn over baldness, an avid follower of Christy
Ring; a clock, a spiral iron staircase to the Gents, the cold of
marble on the wristbone, footsteps passing outside in summer,

the sound of heavy rain falling before closing time. The few times they had met in recent years they had both spoken of nothing but people and happenings, as if those early meetings were some deep embarrassment: that they had leaned on them too heavily once and were now like lost strength.

He rang. The number was that of a small hotel on the quays. Mary Kelleher answered. He invited her to lunch and they arranged to meet in the hotel foyer. He walked to the hotel, and as he walked he felt again the heady, unreal feeling of moving in an unblemished morning, though it was now past midday.

When she rose to meet him in the foyer, he saw that she was as tall as he. A red kerchief with polka dots bound her blonde hair. She was too strong boned to be beautiful but her face and skin glowed. They talked about James White. She had met him at a party in New York. 'He said that I must meet you if I was going to Dublin. I was about to check out of the hotel when you rang.' She had relations in Dundalk that she intended to look up and Trinity College had manuscripts she wanted to see. They walked up Dame Street and round by the Trinity Railings to the restaurant he had picked in Lincoln Place. She was from Mount Vernon, New York, but had been living in Chicago, finishing her doctorate in medieval poetry at the University of Chicago. There were very pale hairs on the brown skin of her legs and her leather sandals slapped as she walked. When she turned her face to his, he could see a silver locket below the line of the cotton dress.

Bernardo's door was open on to the street, and all but two of the tables were empty.

'Everybody's out of town for the holiday. We have the place to ourselves.' They were given a table for four just inside the door. They ordered the same things, melon with Parma ham, veal Milanese, a carafe of chilled white wine. He urged her to have more, to try the raspberries in season, the cream cake, but she ate carefully and would not be persuaded.

'Do you come here often?' she asked.

'Often enough. I work near here, round the corner, in Kildare Street. An old civil servant.'

'You don't look the part at all, but James White did say you worked in the civil service. He said you were quite high up,' she smiled teasingly. 'What do you do?'

'Nothing as exciting as medieval poetry. I deal in law, industrial law in particular.'

'I could imagine that to be quite exciting.'

'Interesting maybe, but mostly it's a job – like any other.'

'Do you live in the city, or outside?'

'Very near here. I can walk most places, even walk to work.' And when he saw her hesitate, as if she wanted to ask something and did not think it right, he added, 'I have a flat. I live by myself there, though I was married once.'

'Are you divorced? Or am I allowed to ask that?'

'Of course you are. Divorce isn't allowed in this country. We are separated. For something like twenty years now we haven't laid eyes on one another. And you? Do you have a husband or friend?' he changed the subject.

'Yes. Someone I met at college, but we have agreed to separate for a time.'

There was no silence or unease. Their interest in one another already far outran their knowledge. She offered to split the bill but he refused.

'Thanks for the lunch, the company,' she said as they faced one another outside the restaurant.

'It was a pleasure,' and then he hesitated and asked, 'What are you doing for the afternoon?' not wanting to see this flow that was between them checked, though he knew to follow it was hardly wise.

'I was going to check tomorrow's trains to Dundalk.'

'We could do that at Westland Row around the corner. I was wondering if you'd be interested in going out to the sea where the world and its mother is in this weather?'

'I'd love to,' she said simply.

It was with a certain relief that he paid the taxi at the Bull Wall. Lately the luxury and convenience of a taxi had become for him the privilege of being no longer young, of being cut off from the people he had come from, and this was exasperated by the glowing young woman by his side, her eager responses to each view he pointed out, including the wired-down palms along the front.

'They look so funny. Why is it done?'

'It's simple. So that they will not be blown away in storms. They are not natural to this climate.'

He took off his tie and jacket as they crossed the planks of
the wooden bridge, its legs long and stork-like in the retreated
tide. The rocks that sloped down to the sea from the Wall were
crowded with people, most of them in bathing costumes,
reading, listening to transistors, playing cards, staring out to
sea, where three tankers appeared to be nailed down in the
milky distance. The caps of the stronger swimmers bobbed far
out. Others floated on their backs close to the rocks, crawled in
sharp bursts, breast-stroked heavily up and down a parallel
line, blowing like walruses as they trod water.

'I used to swim off these rocks once. I liked going in off the
rocks because I've always hated getting sand between my toes.
Those lower rocks get covered at full tide. You can see the tidal
line by the colour.'

'Don't you swim anymore?'

'I haven't in years.'

'If I had a costume I wouldn't mind going in.'

'I think you'd find it cold.'

She told him of how she used to go out to the ocean at the
Hamptons with her father, her four brothers, their black sheep
Uncle John who had made a fortune in scrap metal and was
extremely lecherous. She laughed as she recounted one of
Uncle John's adventures with an English lady.

When they reached the end of the Wall, they went down to
the Strand, but it was so crowded that they had to pick their
way through. They moved out to where there were fewer
people along the tide's edge. It was there that she decided to
wade in the water, and he offered to hold her sandals. As he
walked with her sandals, a phrase came without warning from
the book he had been reading in Webb's: 'What is he doing
with his life, we say: and our judgement makes up for the
failure to realize sympathetically the natural process of living.'
He must indeed be atrophied if a casual phrase could have
more presence for him than this beautiful young woman, and
the sea, and the day. The dark blue mass of Howth faced the
motionless ships on the horizon, seemed to be even pushing
them back.

'Oh, it's cold,' she shivered as she came out of the water,
and reached for her sandals.

'Even in heatwaves the sea is cold in Ireland. That's Howth

ahead – where Maud Gonne waited at the station as Pallas
Athena.' He reached for his role as tourist guide.

'I know that line,' she said and quoted the verse. 'Has all that
gone from Dublin?'

'In what way?'

'Are there . . . poets . . . still?'

'Are there poets?' he laughed out loud. 'They say the standing
army of poets never falls below ten thousand in this unfortunate
country.'

'Why unfortunate?' she said quickly.

'They create no wealth. They are greedy and demanding.
They hold themselves in very high opinion. Ten centuries ago
there was a national convocation, an attempt to limit their
powers and numbers.'

'Wasn't it called *Drum* something?'

'*Drum Ceat*,' he added, made uneasy by his own attack.

'But don't you feel that they have a function – beyond
wealth?' she pursued.

'What function?'

'That they sing the tired rowers to the hidden shore?'

'Not in the numbers we possess here, one singing down the
other. But maybe I'm unkind. There are a few.'

'Are these poets to be seen?'

'They can't even be hidden. Tomorrow evening I could show
you some of the pubs they frequent. Would you like that?'

'I'd like that very much,' she said, and took his hand. A whole
day was secured. The crowds hadn't started to head home yet,
and they travelled back to the city on a nearly empty bus.

'What will you do for the rest of the evening?'

'There's some work I may look at. And you? What will you
do?'

'I think I'll rest. Unpack, read a bit,' she smiled as she raised
her hand.

He walked slowly back, everything changed by the petty
confrontation in Webb's, the return to the flat, the telegram in
the hallway. If he had not come back, she would be in Dundalk
by now, and he would be thinking about finding a hotel for the
night somewhere round Rathdrum. In the flat, he went through
notes that he had made in preparation for a meeting he had with
the Minister the coming week. They concerned an obscure

section of the Industries Act. Though they were notes he had
made himself he found them extremely tedious, and there came
on him a restlessness like that which sometimes heralds illness.
He felt like going out to a cinema or bar, but knew that what he
really wanted to do was to ring Mary Kelleher. If he had learned
anything over the years it was the habit of discipline. Tomorrow
would bring itself. He would wait for it if necessary with his
mind resolutely fixed on its own blankness, as a person prays
after fervour has died.

'Section 13, paragraph 4, states clearly that in the event of
confrontation or disagreement . . .' he began to write.

The dress of forest green she was wearing when she came down
to the lobby the next evening caught his breath; it was
shirtwaisted, belling out. A blue ribbon hung casually from her
fair hair behind.

'You look marvellous.'

The Sunday streets were empty, and the stones gave out a
dull heat. They walked slowly, loitering at some shop windows.
The doors of all the bars were open, O'Neills and the
International and the Olde Stand, but they were mostly empty
within. There was a sense of a cool dark waiting in Mooney's, a
barman arranging ashtrays on the marble. They ordered an
assortment of sandwiches. It was pleasant to sit in the
comparative darkness, and eat and sip and watch the street, and
to hear in the silence footsteps going up and down Grafton
Street.

It was into this quiet flow of the evening that the poet came, a
large man, agitated, without jacket, the shirt open, his thumbs
hooked in braces that held up a pair of sagging trousers, a
brown hat pushed far back on his head. Coughing harshly and
pushing the chair around, he sat at the next table.

'Don't look around,' McDonough leaned forward to say.

'Why?'

'He'll join us if we catch his eye.'

'Who is he?'

'A poet.'

'He doesn't look like one.'

'That should be in his favour. All the younger clerks that work
in my place nowadays look like poets. He is the best we have.

He's the star of the place across the road. He's practically
resident there. He must have been thrown out.'

The potboy in his short white coat came over to the poet's
table and waited impassively for the order.

'A Powers,' the order came in a hoarse, rhythmical voice. 'A
large Powers and a pint of Bass.'

There was more sharp coughing, a scraping of feet, a sigh,
muttering, a word that could have been a prayer or a curse. His
agitated presence had more the sound of a crowd than the single
person sitting in a chair. After the potboy brought the drinks
and was paid, the poet swung one leg vigorously over the other,
and with folded arms faced away towards the empty doorway.
Then, as suddenly, he was standing in front of them. He had his
hand out. There were coins in the hand.

'McDonough,' he called hoarsely, thrusting his palm forward.
'Will you get me a packet of Ci-tanes from across the road?' he
mispronounced the brand of French cigarettes so violently that
his meaning was far from clear.

'You mean the cigarettes?'

'Ci-tanes,' he called hoarsely again. 'French fags. Twenty. I'm
giving you the money.'

'Why don't you get them here?'

'They don't have them here.'

'Why don't you hop across yourself?'

'I'm barred,' he said dramatically. 'They're a crowd of
ignorant, bloody apes over there.'

'All right. I'll get them for you.' He took the coins but instead
of rising and crossing the road he called the potboy.

'Would you cross the road for twenty Gitanes for me, Jimmy?
I'd cross myself but I'm with company,' and he added a large tip
of his own to the coins the poet had handed over.

'It's against the rules, sir.'

'I know, but I'd consider it a favour,' and they both looked
towards the barman behind the counter, who had been
following every word and move of the confrontation. The
barman nodded that it was all right, and immediately bent his
head down to whatever he was doing beneath the level of the
counter, as if to disown his acquiescence.

Jimmy crossed, was back in a moment with the blue packet.

'You're a cute hoar, McDonough. You're a mediocrity. It's no wonder you get on so well in the world,' the poet burst out in a wild fury as he was handed the packet, and he finished his drinks in a few violent gulps, and stalked out, muttering and coughing.

'That's just incredible,' she said.

'Why?'

'You buy the man his cigarettes, and then get blown out of it. I don't understand it.'

'It wasn't the cigarettes he wanted.'

'Well, what did he want?'

'Reassurance, maybe, that he still had power, was loved and wanted after having been turfed out across the way. I slithered round it by getting Jimmy here to go over. That's why I was lambasted. He must have done something outrageous to have been barred. He's a tin god there. Maybe I should have gone over after all.'

'Why didn't you?'

'Vanity. I didn't want to be his messenger boy. He could go and inflate his great mouse of an ego somewhere else. To hell with him. He's always trouble.' She listened in silence as he ended. 'Wouldn't it be pleasant to be able to throw people their bones and forget it?'

'You might have to spend an awful lot of time throwing bones if the word got around,' she smiled as she sipped her glass of cider.

'Now that you've seen the star, do you still wish to cross the road and look in on the other pub?'

'I'm not sure. What else could we do?'

'We could go back to my place.'

'I'd like that. I'd much prefer to see how you live.'

'Why don't we look in across the road, have one drink if it's not too crowded,' and he added some coins to the change still on the table. 'It was very nice of them to cross for the Gitanes. They're not supposed to leave their own premises.'

The door of the bar across the way was not open, and when he pushed it a roar met them like heat. The bar was small and jammed. A red-and-blue tint from a stained glass window at the back mixed weirdly with the white lights of the bar, the light of evening from the high windows. A small fan circled helplessly overhead, its original white or yellow long turned to ochre by cigarette smoke. Hands proffered coins and notes across

shoulders to the barmen behind the horseshoe counter. Pints
and spirit glasses were somehow eased from hand to hand
across the three-deep line of shoulders at the counter the way
children that get weak are taken out of a crowd. The three
barmen were so busy that they seemed to dance.

'What do you think?' he asked.

'I think we'll forget it.'

'I always feel a bit apprehensive going in there,' he admitted
once they were out on the street again.

'I know. Those places are the same everywhere. For a
moment I thought I was in New York at the Cedar Bar.'

'What makes them the same?'

'I don't know. Mania, egotism, vanity, aggression . . . people
searching madly in a crowd for something that's never to be
found in crowds.'

She was so lovely in the evening that he felt himself leaning
towards her. He did not like the weakness. 'I find myself falling
increasingly into an unattractive puzzlement,' he said, 'mulling
over that old, useless chestnut, What *is* life?'

'It's the fact of being alive, I suppose, a duration of time, as
the scholars would say,' and she smiled teasingly. 'Puzzling out
what it is must be part of it as well.'

'You're too young and beautiful to be so wise.'

'That sounds a bit patronizing.'

'That's the last thing I meant it to be.'

He showed her the rooms, the large living-room with the oak
table and worn red carpet, the brass fender, the white marble of
the fireplace, the kitchen, the two bedrooms. He watched her go
over the place, lift the sea shell off the mantelpiece, replace it
differently.

'It's a lovely flat,' she said, 'though Spartan to my taste.'

'I bought the place three years ago. I disliked the idea of
owning anything at first, but now I'm glad to have it. Now,
would you like a drink, or perhaps some tea?'

'I'd love some tea.'

When he returned he found her thumbing through books in
the weakening light.

'Do you have any of the poet's work?'

'You can have a present of this, if you like.' He reached and
took a brown volume from the shelf.

'I see it's even signed,' she said as she leafed through the volume. 'For Patrick McDonough, With love', and she began to laugh.

'I helped him with something once. I doubt if he'd sign it with much love this evening.'

'Thanks,' she said as she closed the volume and placed it in her handbag. 'I'll return it. It wouldn't be right to keep it.' After several minutes of silence, she asked, 'When do you have to go back to your office?'

'Not till Tuesday. Tomorrow is a Bank Holiday.'

'And on Tuesday what do you do?'

'Routine. The Department really runs itself, though many of us think of ourselves as indispensable. In the afternoon I have to brief the Minister.'

'On what, may I ask?'

'A section of the Industries Act.'

'What is the Minister like?'

'He's all right. An opportunist, I suppose. He has energy, certainly, and the terrible Irish gift of familiarity. He first came to the fore by putting parallel bars on the back of a lorry. He did handstands and somersaults before and after speeches, to the delight of the small towns and villages. Miss Democracy thought he was wonderful and voted him in top of the poll. He's more statesmanlike now of course.'

'You don't sound as if you like him very much.'

'We're stuck with one another.'

'Were you upset when your marriage failed?' she changed.

'Naturally. In the end, there was no choice. We couldn't be in the same room together for more than a couple of minutes without fighting. I could never figure out how the fights started, but they always did.'

'Did you meet anyone else?'

'Nothing that lasted. I worked. I visited my parents until they died. Those sort of pieties are sometimes substitutes for life in this country – or life itself. We're back to the old subject and I'm talking too much.'

'No. I'm asking too many questions.'

'What'll you do now that you have your doctorate?'

'Teach. Write. Wait on tables. I don't know.'

'And your husband or friend?'

'Husband,' she said. 'We were married but it's finished. We were too young.'

'Would you like more tea, or for me to walk you back to the Clarence? . . . Or would you like to spend the night here?'

She paused for what seemed an age, and yet it could not have been more than a couple of moments.

'I'd like to spend the night here.'

He did not know how tense his waiting had been until he felt the release her words gave. It was as if blank doors had slid back and he was being allowed again into the mystery of a perpetual morning, a morning without blemish. He knew it by now to be an old con trick of nature, and that it never failed, only deepened the irony and the mystery. 'I'll be able to show you the city tomorrow. You can check out of your hotel then if you wish. And there are the two rooms . . .' he was beginning to say when she came into his arms and sealed his lips.

As he waited for her, the poet's sudden angry accusation came back. Such accusations usually came to rankle and remain long after praise had failed, but not this evening. He turned it over as he might a problem that there seemed no way round, and let it drop. If it was true, there was very little that could be done about it now. It was in turn replaced by the phrase that had come to him earlier by the sea's edge; and had he not seen love in the person of his old mother reduced to noticing things about a farmyard?

'I hope you're not puzzling over something like "life" again,' a teasing call came from the bedroom.

'No. Not this time.' He rose to join her.

In the morning they had coffee and toast in the sunlit kitchen with the expectation of the whole day waiting on them. Then they walked in the empty streets of the city, looked through the Green before going to the hotel to bring her things back to the flat.

The following days were so easy that the only anxiety could be its total absence. The days were heightened by the luxury and pleasure of private evenings, the meals she cooked that were perfection, the good wine he bought, the flowers; desire that was never turned aside or exasperated by difficulty.

At the end of the holiday, he had to go back to the office, and she put off the Dundalk visit and began to go to the Trinity Library. Many people were not back in the office, and he was able to work without interruption for the whole of the first morning. What he had to do was to isolate the relevant parts of the section and reduce them to a few simple sentences.

At the afternoon meeting the Minister was the more nervous. He was tall and muscular, small blue eyes and thick red hair, fifteen years the younger man, with a habit of continually touching anybody close to him that told of the large family he grew up in. They went over and over the few sentences he had prepared until the Minister had them by rote. He was appearing on television that night and was extremely apprehensive.

'Good man,' he grasped McDonough's shoulder with relief when they finished. 'One of these evenings before long you must come out and have a bite with us and meet the hen and chickens.'

'I'll be glad to. And good luck on the TV. I'll be watching.'

'I'll need all the luck I can get. That bitch of an interviewer hates my guts.'

They watched the television debate together in the flat that evening. The Minister had reason to be apprehensive. He was under attack from the beginning but bludgeoning his way. As he watched, McDonough wondered if his work had been necessary at all. He could hardly discern his few sentences beneath the weight of the Minister's phrases. 'I emphatically state . . . I categorically deny . . . I say without any equivocation what-soever . . . Having consulted the best available opinions in the matter,' (which were presumably McDonough's own).

'What did you think?' he asked when he switched off the set.

'He was almost touching,' she said carefully. 'Amateurish maybe. His counterpart in the States might be no better, but he certainly would have to be more polished.'

'He was good at handstands and somersaults once,' he said, surprised at his own sense of disappointment. 'I've become almost fond of him. Sometimes I wish we had better people. They'll all tell him he did powerfully. What'll we do? Would you like to go for a quick walk?'

'Why don't we,' she reached for her cardigan.

Two days later she went to Dundalk, and it wasn't certain how long she intended to remain there. 'I guess I've come so far that they'll expect me to stay over the weekend.'

'You must please yourself. You have a key. I'll not be going anywhere.'

They had come together so easily that the days together seemed like a marriage without any of the apprehension or drama of a ceremony.

When he was young he had desired too much, wanted too much, dreaded and feared too much, and so spread his own fear. Now that he was close to losing everything – was in the direct path of the wind – it was little short of amazing that he should come on this extraordinary breathing space.

Almost in disbelief he went back in reflection to the one love of his life, a love that was pure suffering. In a hotel bedroom in another city, unable to sleep by her side, he had risen and dressed. He had paused before leaving the room to gaze on the even breathing of her sleep. All that breath had to do was frame one word, and a whole world of happiness would be given, but it was forever withheld. He had walked the morning streets until circling back to the hotel he came on a market that was just opening and bought a large bunch of grapes. The grapes were very small and turning yellow and still damp, and were of incredible sweetness. She was just waking when he came back into the room and had not missed him. They ate the grapes on the coverlid and each time she lifted the small bunches to her mouth he remembered the dark of her armpits. He ached to touch her but everything seemed to be so fragile between them that he was afraid to even stir. It seemed that any small movement now could bring calamity. Then, laughing, she blew grape seeds in his face and, reaching out her arms, drew him down. She had wanted their last day together to be pleasant. She was marrying another man. Later he remembered running between airport gates looking for flights that had all departed.

It was eerie to set down those days beside the days that had just gone by, call them by the same name. How slowly those days had moved, as if waiting for something to begin: now all the days were speeding, slipping silently by like air.

Two evenings later, when he let himself into the flat and found Mary Kelleher there, it was as if she had never been away.

'You didn't expect me back so soon?'

'I thought you'd still be in Dundalk, but I'm glad, I'm delighted.' He took her in his arms.

'I had as much of Dundalk as I wanted, and I missed you.'

'How did it go?'

'It was all right. The cousins were nice. They had a small house, crammed with things – religious pictures, furniture, photos. There was hardly place to move. Everything they did was so careful, so measured out. After a while I felt I could hardly breathe. They did everything they possibly could to make me welcome. I read the poems at last,' she put the book with the brown cover on the table. 'I read them again on the train coming back. I loved them.'

'I've long suspected that those very pure love sonnets are all addressed to himself,' McDonough said. 'That was how the "ignorant bloody apes and mediocrities" could be all short-circuited.'

'Some are very funny.'

'I'm so glad you liked them. I've lived with some of them for years. Would you like to go out to eat? Say, to Bernardo's?' he asked.

'I'd much prefer to stay home. I've already looked in the fridge. We can rustle something up.'

That weekend they went together for the long walk in the mountains that he had intended to take the day they met. They stopped for a drink and sandwiches in a pub near Blessington just before two o'clock, and there they decided to press on to Rathdrum and stay the night in the hotel rather than turn back into the city.

It was over dinner in the near empty hotel dining-room that he asked if she would consider marrying him. 'There's much against it. I am fifty. You would have to try to settle here, where you'll be a stranger,' and he went on to say that what he had already was more than he ever expected, that he was content to let it be, but if she wanted more then it was there.

'I thought that you couldn't be married here,' her tone was affectionate.

'I meant it in everything but name, and even that can be arranged if you want it enough.'

'How?'

'With money. An outside divorce. The marriage in some other country. The States, for instance.'

'Can't you see that I already love you? That it doesn't matter? I was half-teasing. You looked so serious.'

'I am serious. I want it to be clear.'

'It is clear and I am glad – and very grateful.'

They agreed that she would spend one week longer here in Dublin than she had planned. At Christmas he would go to New York for a week. She would have obtained her doctorate by then. James White would be surprised. There were no serious complications in sight. They were so tired and happy that it was as if they were already in possession of endless quantities of time and money.

FOR THE BEST IN PAPERBACKS, LOOK FOR THE

In every corner of the world, on every subject under the sun, Penguin represents quality and variety—the very best in publishing today.

For complete information about books available from Penguin—including Pelicans, Puffins, Peregrines, and Penguin Classics—and how to order them, write to us at the appropriate address below. Please note that for copyright reasons the selection of books varies from country to country.

In the United Kingdom: For a complete list of books available from Penguin in the U.K., please write to *Dept E.P., Penguin Books Ltd, Harmondsworth, Middlesex, UB7 0DA.*

In the United States: For a complete list of books available from Penguin in the U.S., please write to *Dept BA, Penguin*, Box 120, Bergenfield, New Jersey 07621-0120.

In Canada: For a complete list of books available from Penguin in Canada, please write to *Penguin Books Canada Ltd, 10 Alcorn Avenue, Suite 300, Toronto, Ontario, Canada M4V 3B2.*

In Australia: For a complete list of books available from Penguin in Australia, please write to the *Marketing Department, Penguin Books Ltd, P.O. Box 257, Ringwood, Victoria 3134.*

In New Zealand: For a complete list of books available from Penguin in New Zealand, please write to the *Marketing Department, Penguin Books (NZ) Ltd, Private Bag, Takapuna, Auckland 9.*

In India: For a complete list of books available from Penguin, please write to *Penguin Overseas Ltd, 706 Eros Apartments, 56 Nehru Place, New Delhi, 110019.*

In Holland: For a complete list of books available from Penguin in Holland, please write to *Penguin Books Nederland B.V., Postbus 195, NL-1380AD Weesp, Netherlands.*

In Germany: For a complete list of books available from Penguin, please write to *Penguin Books Ltd, Friedrichstrasse 10-12, D-6000 Frankfurt Main I, Federal Republic of Germany.*

In Spain: For a complete list of books available from Penguin in Spain, please write to *Longman, Penguin España, Calle San Nicolas 15, E-28013 Madrid, Spain.*

In Japan: For a complete list of books available from Penguin in Japan, please write to *Longman Penguin Japan Co Ltd, Yamaguchi Building, 2-12-9 Kanda Jimbocho, Chiyoda-Ku, Tokyo 101, Japan.*

FOR THE BEST LITERATURE, LOOK FOR THE

☐ **THE BOOK AND THE BROTHERHOOD**
Iris Murdoch

Many years ago Gerard Hernshaw and his friends banded together to finance a political and philosophical book by a monomaniacal Marxist genius. Now opinions have changed, and support for the book comes at the price of moral indignation; the resulting disagreements lead to passion, hatred, a duel, murder, and a suicide pact.   *602 pages*   *ISBN: 0-14-010470-4*

☐ **GRAVITY'S RAINBOW**
Thomas Pynchon

Thomas Pynchon's classic antihero is Tyrone Slothrop, an American lieutenant in London whose body anticipates German rocket launchings. Surely one of the most important works of fiction produced in the twentieth century, *Gravity's Rainbow* is a complex and awesome novel in the great tradition of James Joyce's *Ulysses*.   *768 pages*   *ISBN: 0-14-010661-8*

☐ **FIFTH BUSINESS**
Robertson Davies

The first novel in the celebrated "Deptford Trilogy," which also includes *The Manticore* and *World of Wonders*, *Fifth Business* stands alone as the story of a rational man who discovers that the marvelous is only another aspect of the real.   *266 pages*   *ISBN: 0-14-004387-X*

☐ **WHITE NOISE**
Don DeLillo

Jack Gladney, a professor of Hitler Studies in Middle America, and his fourth wife, Babette, navigate the usual rocky passages of family life in the television age. Then, their lives are threatened by an "airborne toxic event"—a more urgent and menacing version of the "white noise" of transmissions that typically engulfs them.   *326 pages*   *ISBN: 0-14-007702-2*

FOR THE BEST LITERATURE, LOOK FOR THE

☐ **A SPORT OF NATURE**
Nadine Gordimer

Hillela, Nadine Gordimer's "sport of nature," is seductive and intuitively gifted at life. Casting herself adrift from her family at seventeen, she lives among political exiles on an East African beach, marries a black revolutionary, and ultimately plays a heroic role in the overthrow of apartheid.

354 pages   ISBN: 0-14-008470-3

☐ **THE COUNTERLIFE**
Philip Roth

By far Philip Roth's most radical work of fiction, *The Counterlife* is a book of conflicting perspectives and points of view about people living out dreams of renewal and escape. Illuminating these lives is the skeptical, enveloping intelligence of the novelist Nathan Zuckerman, who calculates the price and examines the results of his characters' struggles for a change of personal fortune.

372 pages   ISBN: 0-14-009769-4

☐ **THE MONKEY'S WRENCH**
Primo Levi

Through the mesmerizing tales told by two characters—one, a construction worker/philosopher who has built towers and bridges in India and Alaska; the other, a writer/chemist, rigger of words and molecules—Primo Levi celebrates the joys of work and the art of storytelling.

174 pages   ISBN: 0-14-010357-0

☐ **IRONWEED**
William Kennedy

"Riding up the winding road of Saint Agnes Cemetery in the back of the rattling old truck, Francis Phelan became aware that the dead, even more than the living, settled down in neighborhoods." So begins William Kennedy's Pulitzer-Prize winning novel about an ex-ballplayer, part-time gravedigger, and full-time drunk, whose return to the haunts of his youth arouses the ghosts of his past and present.

228 pages   ISBN: 0-14-007020-6

☐ **THE COMEDIANS**
Graham Greene

Set in Haiti under Duvalier's dictatorship, *The Comedians* is a story about the committed and the uncommitted. Actors with no control over their destiny, they play their parts in the foreground; experience love affairs rather than love; have enthusiasms but not faith; and if they die, they die like Mr. Jones, by accident.

288 pages   ISBN: 0-14-002766-1